The
Redemption of
George Baxter Henry

The
Redemption of
George Baxter Henry

Conor Bowman

THE PERMANENT PRESS
Sag Harbor, NY 11963

"Power of My Love": Recorded by Elvis Presley in February, 1969 at American
    Studios Memphis
Words and Music: Giant/Baum/Kaye
Lyric reprint by kind permission of Elvis Presley Music Publishing

Iska's fridge notes by Hannah Bowman

sourcebooks: *The Book of Apples* by Morgan & Richards, 1993
            The Book of the Apple by H. H. Thomas, 1902

422 0667

For information, address:
    The Permanent Press
    4170 Noyac Road
    Sag Harbor, NY 11963
    www.thepermanentpress.com

Library of Congress Cataloging-in-Publication Data

    Bowman, Conor–
        The redemption of George Baxter Henry / Conor Bowman.
            p. cm.
        "Originally published in 2008 by Clockwork Press of Dublin, Ireland"—
    T.P. verso.
        ISBN 978-1-57962-220-6 (hardcover : alk. paper)
            1. Middle-aged men—Family relationships—Fiction. 2. Midlife
    crisis—Fiction. 3. Dysfunctional families—Travel—Fiction. 4. Americans—
    France—Fiction. 5. Life change events—Fiction. 6. Boston (Mass.)—
    Fiction. 7. France—Fiction. 8. Domestic fiction. I. Title.

    PR6052.O889R43 2011
    823'.914—dc22   2011019985

BIBLIOGRAPHICAL NOTE

The Redemption of George Baxter Henry was originally published in 2008 by
Clockwork Press of Dublin, Ireland.

For George N. Allen (1925–2007)
to whom I am related by ink

ACKNOWLEDGMENTS

I would like to thank Mary Honan, who played an enormous role in bringing George Baxter Henry to life. Without you, Mary, George might not even exist. Lots of love, CB xxx.

Special thanks also to Fiona Keegan (who suggested one crucial revision) and Juliet Bressan (who is as good a friend as you could ever hope to find in a lifetime of looking).

I would also like to express my deepest gratitude to Marty and Judith Shepard, Rania Haditirto, Joslyn Pine, Susan Ahlquist, and everyone else at The Permanent Press, for showing faith in me and my writing.

Hey Dad

Adam's Pearmain;

Indispensible to every collection:

Fairly large, brisk flavor,
A good keeping variety.

Oskar Appleby

CHAPTER ONE

This whole fucking thing starts at twenty-five-thousand feet over the Azores, or some place, with my seventeen-year-old son's head down the toilet. Don't believe me? You better batten down the latches (or whatever the fuck the phrase is) and listen up because every word is absolutely true. This story begins in a john on a 747. The noise was absolutely mind-blowing. People shouting and screaming, and stewards and stewardesses (sometimes there's little enough difference) shooting past each other in the aisles trying to formulate some plan to extricate Billy's head from the toilet bowl.

My son Billy (*our* son—sorry, honey) is a genius. At least that's what he keeps telling us. He plays drums in a college band called East Pole and, in between writing suicidal lyrics and hammering the shit out of his drum kit, he flunks history exams in a two-bit college for social welfare veterans (and other categories of unwanted citizens) in Lansing, Idaho. This should never be confused with the Michigan State capital of the same name. This place is an afterthought belonging to a backwater in the middle of absolutely nowhere you'd ever want to intentionally go or stay. This is the sort of place the word "remote" was invented for. Anyway, with report cards saying "could do better" and straight A's in absenteeism and disinterest, Billy and his prospects were already heading for the toilet even before we caught the plane at JFK. Billy had to be dragged into school on his first day at the age of five and he's still running from education. Like a giant rabbit, who's supposed to like lettuce and carrots but actually prefers cocktails and steak, our son has been kicking against his genes since he was old enough to vomit deliberately. He got into this pathetic repository for educationally challenged drifters because of his scholarship-winning entrance exam. (This scholarship consisted of rooms on campus on a first-come first-served basis at a ten percent reduction. Whoopee!)

The other factor which clinched his place in the course (Bolivian History, 1811–1814) was a fifty-thousand-dollar donation from guess-fucking-who? (You've guessed it). The other benefit for yours truly was a brass plate with my name on a bench in the colonnades outside the college library. The George Baxter Henry seat—rest your ass on that! In a hundred years they'll still be sitting on me, shifting their lard-filled rear ends from side to side and coughing loudly to mask their flatulence. Great! Before you get ahead of yourself and start thinking you're the first to notice it, yes, I am in fact a lawyer and, yes, my initials are GBH! In Europe they find it funny, like in England with the crime of Grievous Bodily Harm and a TV series with the acronym as its title. When you're fifty-one, and have hemorrhoids the size of golf balls every August, your initials are way down the list of priorities, believe you me.

Anyway, Billy had two main problems in the summer of 1999. His band had come to the attention of a major label in New York called Carnivore Records. Sounds great, but there's a snag. Billy was only seventeen and the label wanted his signature, so he needed the consent of his parents. What father could stand in the way of a multi-album deal which might secure his child's financial future? You're looking at him. The second problem Billy had was a little less negotiable than securing my signature—he was a coke addict. Now while most rock stars only go off the rails and burn themselves out after a couple of hits, Billy managed to do all this in advance of even getting the deal. What a trooper! He'd seen the path to riches and was actively practicing one of its primary constituent elements.

Who could thwart the path of such a genius? Once more, look here. On the way to the airport, he was kicking up again about having to come to Europe with us.

"Why can't I stay here and rehearse with the band?"

"What's to rehearse?" I said. "I thought you made it up as you went along."

"In your dreams, Dad. Look, Hairy and Joe are renting this room in New York, like, a rehearsal studio. The label is paying for the whole thing. It's, like, a development deal where we just jam for a couple of hours a day and then when we go in to record the album, they use the tapes as, like, a template for the songs."

"The Beatles used to record a whole album in about forty minutes. They didn't need to blow someone else's budget or rent rehearsal studios in New York."

"That was different, Dad. They had so little time. I mean, studios were hardly invented then. It was rush, rush, rush."

"They had talent, Billy. Don't tell me Sergeant Pepper's was simply the product of lucky studio engineering."

"I bet they didn't have parents who were blocking their paths on the road to stardom."

"I bet their parents didn't have children who snorted more coke than the whole of San Francisco in their first year in college."

"Do we have to go over all of this again, Dad? I told you I've quit, I'm clean."

"You could tell me you're Superman's shrink and I'd believe you sooner."

"You think I'm lying?" His flat nose twitched and I knew he was lying.

"You'd never get that story past a jury," I said.

"How would you know? You haven't fought a trial for thirty years." That was my mother-in-law, Muriel, beside Billy in the back of the limo. We'll get to her later.

"Four weeks of clean urine or no signature, that's the deal. Take it or leave it, Billy."

"I hate France," Billy retorted.

"No, you don't. You hate yourself, you hate mowing the lawn, you hate goat's milk, but you don't hate France. You've never even been there, you know nothing about it."

"I know that I'm gonna hate it. They weren't even in the Vietnam war."

I didn't reply; I was tempted to say something derogatory about Bolivia.

"I am clean," said Billy, folding his arms across a t-shirt that said, VOTE NO TO DEMOCRACY.

"Four weeks, Billy, that's what's required." I closed the subject.

Billy may have been clean in the limo but by the time we hit twenty-five-thousand feet over the Azores, he was at about fifty-thousand feet himself. He tried to escape from the plane via the toilet or something. Anyway, he made the steward's day when he presented a denim rear view to the main aisle of the 747. After he'd been rescued from the john by three of the crew, he was given a sedative and slept for the rest of the journey.

"Has your son taken any non-prescription medication?" a smiling hostess in a horrible red uniform asked politely.

"Oh no, of course not," I replied. "He inhaled the lot from humming an Eric Clapton song by accident. What do you think?"

At best, the four clean weeks would have to start when we landed in Nice. There were a thousand toilets between now and our return flight at the end of September.

The U.S. is a pretty fucked-up place. Everybody knows that. It's a given—like tax return audits and the predisposition of nurses towards casual sex. We have the greatest country in the world; so we're the biggest and the best at everything. We have enormous buildings, the most trailer parks per capita, the craziest TV shows, the most expensive military, and, of course, when it comes to being fucked up we're way out front too. Don't get me wrong, I love my country, I'm just smart enough to realize it doesn't love me back. This whole music thing with Billy has brought it home to me more than ever. I mean, ever since his damn band attracted the mitts of one of the biggest record companies in the world, the phones at Schwartz, McNaghten, Stamp and Henry just hadn't given it a rest. A couple of days before we left for vacation, two of their 'Executive Vice Presidents' came to Boston to plead with me for my signature. Oh yeah, I forgot to tell you, the record company doesn't know squat about the white stuff; they just think Billy has a permanent flu. Figure that out from the country that gave us *Gesundheit* (or was that Peru?).

Anyhow, these two morons land in my office on a Wednesday afternoon of all days (I'll tell you about that later too). They looked like two Mormon evangelizers—Elder Smarter and Elder Younger. They stood on the carpet, shifting their glances from each other back to me. I decided to break the ice.

"Talk to me, fellas. I got a plane to catch on Saturday."

"Mr. Henry." The older guy took up the chase.

"Yes?"

"Carnivore is one of the biggest record companies in the world."

"In the whole world," echoed his partner.

"Now that scares a lot of people."

"Do I look worried?" I grinned. They looked at each other and then back to me again. The younger guy caught the pass and kept running.

"We don't mean that you're scared. What we are saying is that we know you have concerns, and, no matter what those concerns are, we're here to take care of them."

"Yes, and to address them." Jeff followed Mutt. They looked like two guys who had managed to hit the potty for the first time. A satisfied pall settled over them.

"Great," I said. "How are you on environmental-planning code violations?"

They had to figure out, through a series of exchanged shrugs and glances, that this was a joke. They smiled together. I could see that they couldn't see they were getting nowhere. I sent out a few hints.

"Don't miss your train to Logan." They still didn't register.

"Mr. Henry," the now-fatigued older Mormon tried to reopen the conversation, "I suppose you're curious about how a corporation as large as ours can still offer to give every band—"

"—and band member," Dopey helped.

"Yes, of course, and each band member, individual attention and care so as to maximize their longevity as an act and their integrity as an artist?"

The old 'integrity-as-an-artist' line. I was ready to puke. Who the hell did they think would buy baloney in such quantities? Not old GBH, I don't mind telling you.

"Nope, I have no interest in any of that. The whole George Michael thing cleared up all the fuzz around those particular issues for me. There's nothing I want to ask you, no concerns, no paternal worries about how "integrity" and "artist" come to be mixed up in one single phrase you feel like peddling to me in my own office."

"But, surely, you've discussed with Billy how his choice, and of course your choice, may affect the band. Timing is everything in the music industry, I mean what's in vogue today may not even get regional play next week, Mr. Henry."

Elder Smarter tried to play the heavy. He was woofing up the wrong tree.

"Would you say that the U.S. is ahead of Europe as far as music is concerned?" I asked the question in a tone I usually reserved for waitresses who'd got the order wrong.

"Sure, yeah, definitely."

"Ab-so-lutely." Dopey found his echo voice on repeat-sentiment-but-vary-text mode.

"Weeks ahead?"

"Oh sure, I mean, like months, you know?"

"I didn't know that, but I'm delighted to hear it, gentlemen. Because it seems as if East Pole should still be a 'hot ticket' I believe the phrase is, when we meet EMI in Paris on Monday, even if they've already gone out of fashion in New York by then."

I stood up, dismissing them with an extension of my hand for a warm shake. They both bore the 'oh, fuck' expression common to their species when outflanked, and reached for their cell phones simultaneously as they exited the room. I was sure we'd upped the ante on whatever deal they would now offer. Billy would probably never appreciate my actions, even if I could get him to stop lashing his drumskins long enough to think about it.

I called my secretary, Judy, on the intercom.

"Yes, Mr. Henry? I have checked the library for that *LA Times* article in 1930. I've copied it and put one in the safe and the other in your red folder."

"Great, Judy, I'll read it on the plane. But there's something else I need you to do. Get on to Rex Verdmin in London. Ask him to put a call through to Carnivore Records' legal department in New York. Tell him to ask for a copy of East Pole's development deal contract."

"You got it, Mr. Henry."

A bit of interest from London would have them pooping in their Lexus. Same old same old. You know, I hate it when people talk bullshit and pretend it doesn't stink. I overheard some jerk in a restaurant talking about how great Chicago was and how the all-seater stadium was standing room only for the home games. Work that out! Of course, the place is empty for the fucking away games! Duh.

"We have a little joke, like a special thing we say in Chicago. You know, when we're not going to be at the office. We say, 'Oh, I have an appointment with the doctor today'—he winks—'Doctor Wrigley.' He laughs and his companion throws him a look that says either, 'Take me home and bonk me rigid' or, 'What?' He sniggers again and lowers his voice. 'You see, Wrigley is the name of the park and so when you say doctor, I have an appointment at the, "Doctor Wrigley"—wink, wink—everybody knows what you mean.'"

I wonder what people in Chicago say when they're sick and going to see a real doctor? Maybe, "Hey, I got a game to play this afternoon, I'm shortstop down at the hospital." Or some stupid thing like that.

Those two morons from the label ought to meet that prick and they could all go to Dr. Wrigley's together and bore each other instead of me. You got these guys back from the Gulf War, and suddenly their asthma charts make a more interesting topic of conversation than these twits from Chicago, wittering on about the "doctor."

Billy discovered cocaine around the time most teenage boys are swapping *Playboy* for a real grope. Some kid from the other side of the river brought a couple of lines in his knapsack to summer camp and there you go. While other people's children were being busted for taking their old man's car out without a license, Billy was doing lines of coke on top of the dashboard, while his contemporaries were exchanging pieces of ass in the back seat. It got so his nose was red all the time and that's what tipped us off. I mean, the blank stares, the glazed eyes, the lethargy, and the frequent uncontrollable fits of laughing or diarrhea had all been part of Billy's repertoire since third grade, so how were we to know it was drugs? Apparently, half of the stuff is cut with Italian laxatives to give you a run for your money. There's a little piece of Colombia that should have a plaque to Billy Stanislaus Henry, saying, "I'm dreaming of a white Christmas, and Easter and Thanksgiving and Halloween." God bless the cartels and General Noriega.

I suppose I should reveal a little of myself here and say that, on a social level and from the point of view of family aesthetics, I would prefer my kids to do cocaine rather than crack or heroin. At least we were able to give Billy the opportunities we never had ourselves. There were no syringes and shared needles. Out-of-date credit cards and a flat surface were all it took to send Billy on his way. Our family doctor, Dr. Volt of the Cantronelli Medical Centre, put our minds at ease about Billy's addiction.

"He's unlikely to contract AIDS with this habit." This was an enormous consolation to me as a parent. My wife, Pearl, however, was alarmed by the mention of the "A" word.

"AIDS? I thought only homosexual-intravenous-drug-taking Africans could get that." She was as alarmed as a cat that hears of a slump in the value of mouse shares.

"Well, to a degree, you're correct in your analysis, Mrs. Henry." (There was no way he was going to risk losing a twenty-thousand-a-year insurance-plan family like ours.) "Many of the categories of person you've described are indeed in the high risk bracket, but what I'm saying is that Billy is in that particular grouping of . . .'

"Drug addicts?" I suggested.

"Yes, yes. Billy is in a grouping which has a high likelihood of non-contraction."

A 'high likelihood of non-contraction.' What the hell is that for a social category? It sounds like an anti-pregnancy lobby. I thought of Iska, our daughter, named after the Apache word for water because of the associated complications her home birth might have brought. Pearl was pressurized by her mother to try the 'natural method' with our second child, but declined, thank Christ. The 'natural method' is too horrific to go into; but, by way of analogy, it's a bit like inviting your local butcher to slaughter his herd in your front room just so you can have a piece of beef for your Sunday lunch. Ever wondered why there's no such thing as natural dentistry? Anyhow, I digress—back to old Doctor Volt; he, of course, had the perfect solution to Billy's problem.

"There's a clinic in Lebanon, PA, Mr. and Mrs. Henry. It houses a facility called the Youth Outreach Realignment Scheme. Billy would be met at the airport by an addiction marshal who would provide one-on—one buddy contact for the eight-week program which—"

"How much?" I asked, cutting across him.

"How much success? Well, in percentile terms the recidivism rate compares . . ."

"I meant how much does the fucking treatment cost? I don't need to hear how other people's children got on," I snapped.

"Oh." He appeared, for the first time in his life, embarrassed to talk about money. "Thirty-five-thousand dollars," he whispered; and then, remembering the best thing of all about it. "That does include meals."

Let me tell you, I've had it up to fucking here with doctors. The only guarantee every patient of every doctor has is that sooner or later they're gonna die. If every car was definitely gonna crash, who'd ever buy one? I didn't swallow old Voltometer's pitch for that overreaching reassignment thing in Pennsylvania. Let's get it straight: there's very little in my book that medical science can ever hope to achieve with thirty-five-thousand bucks that the average parent can't match with some bulk-bought Tylenol and a little creativity around the house.

When we landed in Nice, the heat rushed up at us from the tarred runways and seeped into the airport through inch-thick glass as we headed for the baggage carousel. Billy was still half asleep, but we managed to balance him on top of the luggage trolley as we headed for the customs post. I saw a policeman with a German shepherd nosing around a couple of people's bags. I immediately panicked and thought of Billy's suitcase. God only knew what he'd packed. I imagined for a moment that the suitcase would be opened to reveal a mountain of white powder which would cover the dog from head to paw as it toppled over under the weight of its one hundred-percent Colombian coat. The dog, I reckoned, was an addict too. He looked at Billy and woofed, and then hung his tongue out to lick Billy's hand. Billy sat there with his own tongue hanging out, and they looked strangely kindred for a few intimate seconds before the tranquility of the airport hum was shattered by the clatter of dozens of silver spoons cascading out of a holdall belonging to a passenger going through the green channel.

"It's not the France I remember," my mother-in-law complained, as two backpackers edged through her rather than around her.

"Of course, it's not," I assisted. "They've got cars now and the Revolution is over." My wife, Pearl, who had not spoken to me for nearly two weeks, suddenly broke her vow of silence.

"Mother is ninety-one, you know, George. I wish you'd try to show some respect for at least one of the girls in this family every once in a while."

"Don't cry, dear," Muriel auto-suggested her daughter into floods of wailing in the most public place you could imagine. "George doesn't mean to be nasty and disloyal, it's just his way." She smiled a grin which tempted me to spit at her, but I was afraid I might miss.

"C'mon, Dad." My daughter tugged at my arm. "Billy's just been sick on the trousers of the metal detector man. I think we should catch up."

"I'm trying," I said; but I was still ever-vigilant in my suspicion that the goons from the record label might have followed us. I looked around—no sign. My mother-in-law was in top form now, smiling inanely at people she thought recognized her from the big screen. My ass they did. Pearl, meanwhile, gave me a look which said, "Get the luggage" and, "Why did we ever marry?" in one fell swoop.

When you plan your own retirement, make sure it doesn't include your family. Half of them will bleed you dry in a second and embarrass you from toilet to arrivals lounge, in any fucking language you care to try; while the other half subject you to the silent treatment for the slightest perceived transgression. At least we'd arrived and were all in one piece. Just as long as Billy's nose stayed attached to his face.

Dad,

Found a great book about cidar apples

'The Mystery of Husbandry Discovered and layd open'.
(from 1675)

Love from gska

CHAPTER TWO

We were pretty late starting a family. I don't deny that. You can't ever be too late starting because, to be honest, children are the cosmic method of reminding you of the frailty of human existence and the inadequacy of man's earning potential. You can lose the run of yourself with a credit card or a checkbook every once in a while, but it's all controllable ultimately; you nip and tuck next month's earnings to compensate and you learn from the experience when there's just you. With children (and a wife who has an equity share in your law firm) it's completely different. It's like having an army of robbers out there with unlimited access to your private finances and absolutely no way of slowing them down. It's like wearing a sign around your neck that says, "My Personal Identification Number is 543210 and, by the way, I'm not home right now, so why don't you call round and trash the fucking house as well." It's actually worse than that, because every night the thieves come home to your house and have their own rooms and enjoy unlimited access to your fridge as well. You know the Catholic kick about never saying you can't afford more children? It's bullshit. Children are the single greatest drain on the world's finances after global warming and oil-slick clean-up costs. The most blatant lawyer/client rip-off is only in the shadows when compared to the financial fraud visited on parents by their children.

Thankfully, Pearl has her limits in the spend department. She's as prone to a crazy bout of retail therapy as the next woman, but she's pretty sensible about it. She knows that if she kicks the golden goose in the balls, eventually the goose may cough up blood instead of dollars. With children, there's no endgame, no realization that the supply is finite. As far as they're concerned, it's win, win, win. They didn't ask to be born so you pay for that. You want the best for them, so you pay for that, and, best of all, they hate you and you want them to love you, so you pay for that too. Stick a dunce hat on me and call me Chase Manhattan! Jeez.

Let me tell you about Iska. She's fourteen and the doctors told us she'd always be a "little slow." What's the big deal with that? I mean traffic from Brooklyn to Central Park is often a "little slow," but it gets there in the end. I never could figure out what they meant by that phrase. Were we to start believing that something was wrong and, if it was, how wrong would that be? Iska was an identical twin, and the other girl died about a day after they were born. We were told that if we'd gone the home-birth route, we'd almost certainly have lost Iska as well. Iska weighed two-and-half pounds and was eight weeks early. Doesn't sound slow to me. It was like she couldn't get here fast enough. Do you know who I think was a "little slow"? The fucking gynecologist. I mean, he told us that it was a single pregnancy. I interpreted the scan and said, "Hey, it looks like two in there." He gave me a look that said, "Fuck you and I know you're a lawyer." But he changed his tune when the assistant, who was, like, only printing out the damn thing, put him right. How big of a moron would someone have to be before you'd let him poke his hands up your wife? What do most of them have, besides a med-school certificate and an office the size of Las Vegas? Very little if you ask me.

Like I said before (I hope), I hate doctors, they're worse than lawyers. At least we don't drop the hand on our clients and then pretend it's all part of the service. Doctors are probably the most depraved bunch of qualified people anywhere. They have the power over life and death. It's just shades of incompetence which decide the details. "A little slow," my joystick.

I do want to make the subtle distinction here between medical negligence and medical negligence lawsuits. One is a reprehensible side effect of an inadequate medical care system, and the other is the legitimate pursuit of constitutional rights by perhaps the last of the truly caring professions. There, I've got that off my chest.

Anyhow, Iska arrived safe and sound, and continues to confound the textbook fucking doom and gloom prophesies that surrounded her entry into our world. In kindergarten, she outshone all of her competitors in that cosseted world of the rules and philosophy of Maria Mussolini, with novel learning methods and endless games of point-out-the-plastic-fruit.

For the last two years or so, Iska's been doing research for a book she intends to write about apples. Every couple of days, she leaves me notes about her latest discovery pinned to the refrigerator by magnets. She signs them, 'Iska Applebee,' so I know who they're from. It's just a thing she does. I mean, half the time I don't understand the notes but I do read them and, yeah, I hang onto them for God knows why. I guess Freud, or even Dr. Volt, would make a connection between those notes and some basic dysfunction in our own household. Find me a family devoid of dysfunction and I'll show you a bunch of lying medics living together in some parallel universe.

Anyway, we land in Nice and, in about thirty seconds, my temperature is higher than Mount fucking Rushmore. The city is bang in the middle of the biggest taxi strike the world has ever seen. There's lines of the bastards sitting in their air-conditioned rip-off mobiles with their engaged signs on and nobody's getting a ride anywhere. I have to say that they're the same the world over, these guys: insidious money-grabbing-know-all-road-ragers in every city or town you visit. Why is it that only people with criminal records and brain damage (that lethal cocktail) are allowed to drive cabs?

"I thought you'd organized a car, George." Mother-in-law kicks the situation closer to the sewer.

"I tried, but they were all out of hearses." I smile.

Pearl gives me the cold shoulder again in the heat. Iska's left us baking on the sidewalk, and she returns a minute later with a smart-looking man in a blue uniform.

"This is Philippe," she says. "He's going to drive us to the place."

"Who is this guy?" Billy wakes up for the first time in about two months.

"He's a driver from one of the hotels in Monte Carlo. He's just finished for the weekend and he'd love a bit of private work." Iska smiles at the cute guy from Monte Carlo and then talks in some strange language. (It has to be French.) We all hit the sidewalk with our jaws, and then he starts loading the bags back onto a trolley and indicates for to us to follow him. About fifty yards down behind the Neanderthal cab strike he's got a minibus. He packs the trunk with our collective junk and opens the door of the bus for us. Cool manufactured air whacks us and Billy looks like he's just done a line.

"This is worse than LA," the ninety-one-year-old witch remarks as we become stuck in traffic just outside the airport. This is a swipe at me because I'm from LA. Nobody ever admits to being from LA (except me). Everyone is either from Jersey and just passing through, or they're from San Jose and waitressing their way to an Oscar. Me? I'm from LA and proud of it.

We edge out of the traffic and across some motorway junction, and suddenly we're in the country with scorched grass and signs for Antibes. We're heading north and away from the sea. Maybe this is a good time to tell you a few things about LA and our family.

My mother-in-law, Muriel Hale, was a movie star in the twenties and thirties. She was nominated for an Oscar as Best Supporting Actress in 1930 but, thank Christ (and the Academy), she didn't win. The film was called, *Turn Left at Brooklyn Bridge*, and was a box-office flop. Muriel starred opposite some poor unfortunate called William Craw who was never heard of again. God only knows how she got the nomination, but, anyway, she never stops telling us about it. Born plain old Muriel Meek, she changed her name to copper-fasten her star status. I never heard of anyone so inappropriately maiden-named as Muriel Meek. She's about as goddamned meek as a Panzer division. When those bible people said the meek would take over the world, I bet most people thought they were kidding. To get a clear picture of my precious mother-in-law in your head, think Godzilla meets Margaret Thatcher and they have a child! I bet the whole movie industry got shivers up its ass when she was nominated for an Oscar. Muriel wears so much makeup now she'd be a shoo-in for an award for special effects.

So the thing about LA is that she lived there for movie star reasons. But I'm from there, so she looks down on me. The stuck-up cricket, who does she think she is? So, any time she can she puts LA down and, with it, yours truly.

"Elvis had a house in LA," I remark, as a comeback to her comment at the airport half an hour earlier. "Family is family." She doesn't take the bait, but looks at Pearl and shakes her head to convey thirty years of mother-in-law disappointment. The driver picks up on the Elvis reference and asks Iska if she likes Elvis Presley. She grins a 'yes' back and he touches the button on the CD player: "Suspicious Minds." Absolutely fantastic. I sing along.

Muriel's husband Louie, who died in 1970, was a third cousin twice-removed of Elvis's father's (Vernon) second wife: Dee Stanley. It was about as far removed as you could be, but it absolutely infuriated Pearl's mother because it meant that there was a rival genetic line to greatness in the family.

Muriel detested mention of the singer and became particularly irate at any reference to the family connection. None of us had ever met Elvis, but Pearl and I saw him in concert in Indianapolis in 1977. I told Muriel once that I'd sent a note to Elvis, via the concert promoter, telling him some relatives were in the audience and mentioning her name just to press home the advantage. Elvis died shortly afterwards and I often told Muriel not to blame herself.

"He probably just couldn't live with the fact that there was another huge star in the family," I said one Christmas Day, helping things along in the seasonal spirit.

"Don't patronize me, George," she retorted. "He was never nominated for an Oscar was he?"

"No, but he probably got paid a lot more for each movie than you made in an entire career spanning, what would it be, eighty years?"

"Twenty years. I gave up the screen because I wanted to concentrate on my family."

"Perhaps you should have ignored them a little more, Muriel. Maybe they'd have turned out normal."

"Normal? What is normal, George? A man who spends years qualifying as a lawyer and then develops trial-phobia? Is that normal, George?"

Of course, I'd never sent a note to the King at the concert at all but, from time to time, I'd reverse-revive the story and start blaming myself for his death. That drove her bananas. We had a dog for about ten years whose real name was Chirpy, but whom I insisted on calling Old Shep. It drove Muriel crazy to be reminded of the Elvis 'connection,' so you can take my word that I never missed an opportunity to do just that. One year I rang every Elvis Fan Club I could find through a business name search, and asked them to mail a membership form to Muriel. It got so she began to rip up her mail without even opening it and destroyed at least one check from her retirement policy. We don't really get on.

I have one brother called Paul Cézanne Henry and he lives in Detroit where he runs an auto repair dealership. The thing is, my mom saw a painting by Van Gogh which she hated in some bridal magazine, and set about trying to find a name for her new arrival which would be a statement against Van Gogh! What was that all about? Van Gogh probably wasn't even alive in the 1950's. Dad died in 1956 of old age at thirty-eight. (That's what they told me, and it was never clarified.) I never knew him really. My mom got a heart attack and died in the Cedar Sinai Hospital while visiting a neighbor who subsequently made a full recovery. For obvious reasons, our family never entered flower shows or crossword competitions. At my mom's funeral some horrible priest who didn't know her at all gave a sermon in which he kept referring to her as 'Karen' (her name was Katherine). So there's a fair quantity of death in our families, but very little of it in the zones I'd hoped for. Muriel looks like she'll live another couple of hundred years. In a way, I couldn't care less if she outlived me. At least I'd have a couple of quiet years before she joined me in Hell.

Pearl. Well, where do I start? We met at a high school in Malibu and dated for a while, then broke up and didn't meet for another ten or twelve years. We married when we were both on the rebound, so you can imagine the combined velocity there. She'd been to college in Wyoming and had majored in sewing or something. Maybe that's unfair, since it was domestic economics with a final year thesis on the role of knitting in Government Defense budgeting. We met up again in a bar in Los Angeles she'd escaped to when she was accompanying her mother to the Oscar ceremony, where everyone who'd made Schlockbuster failures in the previous two hundred years was invited for cocktails and a chance to see some real talent pick up their awards.

We got married in Palm Springs, and Lucille Ball was the only real celebrity at the wedding besides Muriel. Gregory Peck was supposed to come, but he was at a film festival somewhere in Europe promoting *The Omen*. Maybe he could have worked his exorcizing skills on Muriel. We'll never know now. We moved to Boston in '79 and I became a partner in Schwartz, McNaghten and Stamp in 1982, the year that Billy was born. When Iska arrived in 1985 she was a bit of a surprise, but then what pregnancy isn't a surprise? Plus, we were lucky to have her at all, with the twin stuff I mentioned earlier. Pearl and I got on well for most of the time; and when I needed money to outbid Herby Dykeman for partner, Muriel advanced her daughter most of her inheritance in exchange for a cash payola of a sum equal to sixty percent of my share in the firm, on top of alimony, if we ever got divorced (Muriel's idea). It sounded like a good deal for me at the time. I was young and in debt, you know what I mean?

I've heard people say that the reason a bride smiles walking down the aisle is because she knows she'll never have to give another blow job in her entire life. I can't agree with that, but I will say that Pearl grinned broadly on the return flight from our honeymoon in Hawaii, and I'm now re-evaluating the genesis of her contentment. What can I say? You marry in good faith, you gel in good times, and every now and then, when the cracks appear, you paper them over with a mixture of realism and regret and get fucking on with it. At least that's the theory. We've been through a lot together and we're twenty-three years married last April. We have two cars and a summerhouse in Martha's Vineyard. Some bastard reintroduced skunks to the island some time ago, and now you walk around on tiptoe waiting for the fucking stink to appear. Then you have to bathe your dog in tomato juice to get rid of the smell.

Anyway, skunks aside, we make the best of our stays on the Vineyard, spending a little time together. Usually it works, but over the years the fireworks have taken a bit longer each summer to dry out and stoke up, if you know what I mean? Three years ago we reached the breaking point when Billy threw an axe at a skunk from the upstairs window and missed—but killed the Labrador next door. Now the neighbor's place is up for sale and the emotional distress of their kids is the subject of litigation. That's what I call an abuse of the legal system. Why didn't they just have the funeral and then buy another mutt? Some people, all they want is to extend their own grief and wallow in it by flashback for as long as they fucking can. Needless to say, their over-reaction impinged on our stay as well, and suddenly it's the freeze-out from them, and Pearl and I find ourselves having to justify Billy to everybody, including himself.

"Dad, do you think dogs go to heaven?" (This was before he discovered cocaine, if you can credit it.)

"You mean what will happen to Grandma when she dies?"

"No, the dog next door."

"The lady whose mutt you beheaded?"

"No, no, Dad. I mean the fucking Labrador."

"Don't use language like that when your grandmother's not around. I told you once, I've told you a million times, Billy."

What I'm really saying about Pearl is that, well, frankly, we stopped having sex about five years ago. There have been a couple of incidents of congress since; but usually we fly solo and sleep soundly. I don't think she misses it at all and, as each year passed, I was kinda forgetting what it all looked or felt like myself too. People say marriage isn't all roses, but I'd go further and say it's mostly bills and parent/teacher meetings with a little pasta and misunderstanding thrown in. What keeps people together? What drives them apart? Damned if I know.

This family trip to France was planned on short notice. The catalyst was really a single incident about a month earlier when Pearl found out that I was having an affair, every Wednesday afternoon, with one of the girls in the translation service on the ninth floor of the building where Schwartz, McNaghten, Stamp and Henry bill clients by the hour. Now, I know a lot of people run the stock excuses about extramarital sex (or in my case just sex) when they're caught, like, "she means nothing to me" or, "I'm sorry, honey, it's not that there's something wrong with you; this is about me." Take it from me; that's wholesale bullshit at a knockdown price. As far as I'm concerned, I went elsewhere to get something that had dried up at home. It was either that or sleazy cinemas and hookers. So I chose the hump-kitten from the translation service on the ninth floor.

If I'm so goddamn frank about the reasons for my infidelity, why didn't I have the balls (don't even go there) to tell Pearl about it before she found out? The oldest reason in the world: the fear of having a divorce court trigger the post-nuptial equity sale bargain struck when I became partner. (Well, maybe not verbatim the oldest reason in the world, but close.) Was I putting her feelings first and hoping that what she didn't know wouldn't bother her? Absolutely not. If it weren't for the money thing, I'd have walked out on Pearl after the Ark docked. Naw, scratch that. Sure, I had feelings for her, but maybe sometimes people just drift apart and, by the time you notice it, they're outta sight. Who knows?

How did Pearl find out about the affair? Take a guess. Old prehistoric Miss Marple suspected something was going on and, to protect her daughter's honor, hired a private detective to sneak around behind my back and do the dirty on me. How low is that? So she obtains a couple of snapshots and next thing an envelope appears at breakfast. Pearl and Muriel sit at the other end of the table, one crying, the other gloating (you figure who's who). I open the flap and a shot of my own ass greets me, poking away at Gloria who is fluent in Greek and Urdu. It's not the most flattering image of me available in the known world, but it does the trick. I turn the photo upside down and feign confusion for as long as I think I can get away with it.

"Pearl wants a divorce, George." Muriel smirks.

"No I don't," Pearl says, sobbing.

"Shut up, Pearl. She wants a divorce."

It's clear who's in the driver's seat here. I don't even dare try the 'I-can-explain-routine.' What's to explain? My ass is in the air and in pretty good focus.

"Now, George." Muriel sniffs the air to convey measured disappointment rather than anger. "You have two choices. One: you can move out today and nominate a firm to handle the divorce for you and sort out Pearl's sixty percent share of your partnership holding, plus alimony and child support and leave the family home or . . . two: you ditch the twenty-year-old tongue queen and attend counseling with a mediator to save your marriage."

"What was option one again?" I ask. Pearl shifts the sobbing into fifth gear and her mom puts an arm around her shoulders in a gesture that says, 'I won't let the rabid dog near you.' So, we do counseling.

The prick attempting to superglue our relationship back together looks like a Chinese version of Bill Gates. From the get-go, I sense that he may be an even bigger prick than he looks.

"Have either of you ever used sex toys? Or, 'sex aids' as they're known in the trade."

"Which trade?" I ask. "The sex toy industry or counseling?" Pearl is embarrassed. It's hard to gauge why exactly, but old mediator-counselor-accuser is not about to give in.

"No one enjoys a joke more than myself, George. But unless we are all focused on goals here, I won't be able to help you and Earl get through your problems."

"Pearl," I corrected.

"Excuse me?"

"Her name is Pearl, not Earl. It's like the oyster thing. Okay?"

He ignored my admonition and we were right back in jargonsville with vibrators and blow-up dolls. He continued in the intrusive question vein and eventually, when we'd established that neither of us had used them, David (Yong) produced some samples from a drawer and ran through each by description, like he was telling us how to assemble an inhaler or giving the safety speech on an aircraft.

"This is a multi-speed vibrator," he said, as he picked up a gold-colored slim model which looked like a cigar holder. He switched it on and it sat there on the table buzzing like a wasp and twitching slowly like an uncertain compass. We saw various shapes and sizes and contraptions and equipment with enough straps and buckles to outfit a herd of greyhounds. By the end of the first half hour, the table was barely visible under the weight of buzzing vibrators and fur-lined handcuffs. Whatever happened to good old straight sex? I was exhausted looking at the stuff and, instead of seeing ideas to spice up our lives back home and getting turned on in any way, I began to wonder if in fact the whole collection actually belonged to Mr. Yong for his own gratification.

We discussed my infidelity and I was encouraged to "own" my behavior.

"Of course I own it," I replied. "I'm talking about my own infidelity. How can that not be mine?" Ownership apparently was a couple of steps ahead of that place.

"We can have something belong to us and yet not own it," David, the prick, said patronizingly, with a smile which revealed expensive dental care.

"Oh, I see, like listening but not hearing," I threw out the line. He grabbed it and sent it racing up his ass with the buzzes and twitches.

"Ex-act-ly, George. That is ex-act-ly what I mean."

"Like looking but not seeing." I pushed the boat right out into the rapids.

David Yong leaned forward towards us and, resting his elbows on the table between some handcuffs and double-headed dildos, tapped his fingertips and said, "We are all in the same zone now. Let's move forward together shall we? Stepping carefully to avoid the traps and hazards, we can push through to the other side."

"Ouch," I thought, looking at the armory on the table.

Two weeks of daily sessions with that pervert and I was ready to 'own' Mount-fucking-Everest. He stiffed us (me) for eight thousand bucks and sent us on our way with a mock-up diploma each which read: *I'm making the grade in listening but I need a distinction in hearing to continue to graduate in my relationship.*

Our final task was to promise to take a holiday together immediately. "No cell phones," were the prick's last words of advice, and it was about the only thing he'd said in two weeks which made sense to me. (Although hardly eight thousand dollars' worth.) Pearl insisted on Europe (to get away from "that woman in the translation service"). Muriel insisted on coming to protect her daughter, but dressed it up as some doctor's advice to spend more time with her family. How much more time with us did she need? I mean, she fucking lives with us. I imagined her playing the martyr and offering to stay at home on her own, except for some recent sharp pains in her chest and a desire to help save our marriage. Such a thought gave me about as much comfort as I would have derived from finding Himmler in our garage reading the gas meter.

We couldn't let Billy out of our sight for more than twenty minutes in case he overdosed, so he came as well. Iska was too young to leave in Boston on her own, plus she was probably the only one who'd talk to me, so I was happy to have her along. A friend of mine in a travel agency in Harvard Square found the ideal venue. It was a small chateau, or manor house, in Provence, a six-week deal (including a housekeeper and meals) and an option to purchase at the end of our stay. We didn't speak French, but then that's not a problem for Americans; all we do is shout (or overthrow the local regime) in order to be understood whenever we're abroad.

"Here it is," Iska yelled, as we drove in a haze of dust past some olive groves and fields of vines. Red-tiled roofs and white walls gleamed in the afternoon sun. I put my hand in my pocket to feel for the slip of paper with the key-pad combination on it. Instead, I found a fax which had arrived in my office as I was leaving. I'd have to put that in the red folder before I forgot.

Someone in the bus laid a silent one which gave the air-conditioning a good run for its money!

Get This,

The best spot to grow fruit
is on a south-faceing
gentle slope, open to the sun
sheltered from wind and where
the frost does not gather

   but filters down
   and
   away.

        Iska

CHAPTER THREE

I don't know how long the French lasted against the Germans in the Second World War. Maybe six days, but it's not clear whether that included a weekend. They've got some fucking unbelievable country, you know. They blocked our troops from using their air space during the Gulf War and, at the same time, expected us to continue buying goat's cheese. What the hell was that all about? I tell you, they were glad to see us twice in the last hundred years, when the Germans kicked their asses, but they don't want to see us at all when we're saving someone else in the Middle or Central East, or whatever, and preserving the price of oil. Last time I bought goat's cheese, it was in a jar full of fucking oil! Figure that out. They're a country founded on the twin pillars of petulant shrugs and incomprehensible cinema techniques. No wonder they don't have the stomach for war.

So, we arrive in the village, Gigondas (you do pronounce the "ass" at the end), and there's the house we're renting for six weeks to save our marriage (thanks to Mr. Vibrator). It's about a thousand years old and made of stone (like Hillary Clinton), and it's perched at the edge of a tiny village (no shopping malls) and overshadowed by a set of mountains which look like false teeth. It's hot, it's dry, it's dusty and it's August. But it's also kinda pretty, in that sparse European way. We haven't seen a McDonalds since Nice and, in a way, that's comforting. It means that France can survive in the kitchen on its own if it puts a little thought into it. Don't get me wrong, I know they're famous for their chefs and all that, but, to be fair, most of it is just hype; like the "Avenue Du Roi" in Boston near the wharves. You gotta book there three months in advance and binge eat for about the same length, given the microscopic fucking portions they serve. They leave the microscope in the kitchen when they make up the bill though; you can see that from about two hundred yards. They even leave a space for tips, like they do in France. I remember once, a couple of months after I was made partner, we went there and Ivel Schwartz wrote, "thanks a bunch" in the space. That may seem pretty tame to you as far as outrage goes, but, let me tell you, it's pretty extreme from a guy whose response to Watergate was, "Well, well, well." You have to refinance your mortgage at the door just to be allowed in to eat their tiny portions of lettuce and mint bay-leaf roulade or whatever. You wouldn't want to arrive there hungry. That's all I can say.

This village hadn't changed in years, I'd bet. There was a small square with a few wine shops and a phone booth, also a tourist advice center that always seemed to be closed. There was a pair of churches, one small hotel, a couple of cafes, some winding streets, and that's about it. Everywhere, there was the scent of perfume, like they had litres of lavender oil and sprayed it on the fields. Hell, they probably even grow the stuff, although I didn't see any oil derricks. There were lots of vineyards, all gathered around the outside of the village. The houses were mostly roofed in red tiles. The mountain range loomed behind the village. I'll say this for the place though, it was awfully quiet and serene.

The holiday house was absolutely magical. It had a charm that superimposed itself on you even if you were determined to be miserable. I wasn't miserable, but I did kinda hope that some rotting beams might collapse the laundry room on Pearl's mother. But, of course, nothing like that happened. Muriel grabbed the largest bedroom, while Pearl and I had two rooms with a linking door in case we got back together. Iska had a single which had a huge oak windowsill with the initials CA carved in faint ridges near the left inside window sash. Billy's room was downstairs in a converted back kitchen. I'd phoned ahead some days earlier and got Gloria to put her limited French to good use by giving a couple of customizing tips to the agent handling the rental. He'd said that the house had been attached to a vineyard at some stage, but the fields nearest to it now were just dirt and dust. Gloria's final act of sensuousness towards me was to apply lipstick to her adventurous mouth in the aftermath of our last Wednesday ration of passion, three days before I boarded the plane for France. It was going to be tough on her, having me so far away from her for a month and a half, and I told her so.

"Don't go crazy on the credit card, okay, Gloria? The limit is right down to four thousand a month while I'm away."

"George, you make me feel like a hooker, talking about money like that. It's as if my bank account only goes up with your pecker."

"Inflation is a curse, Gloria. You need a little lull every now and then to remind you how good it is to be taken care of. How could you think of yourself as a hooker? I'm absolutely shocked to think you only want my body because I'm paying for you to have sex with me. Haven't you any feelings for me at all?"

"Of course, I have, George. It's just that sometimes I feel cheap about this arrangement."

"Cheap? Are you fucking joking? If I shelled out this kind of money on real hookers, I'd own half of Thailand by now. Whatever you are, honey, 'cheap' ain't it."

I don't mean to be down on Gloria (apart from in the sexual sense), but any commercial deal has to be two-way. Sure, if it develops into something more, I'm open to that. Let's face it, I'm no oil painting. But a bunch of real estate and cash-on-hand is better than a few pastels when you're fifty-one. The sex with Gloria was great. I mean, really great. People often talk about true love and fulfillment and happiness, and all that shit, but, take it from me, money can buy it all. If you're hoping I'll say that every Wednesday I came away from Gloria's apartment feeling empty and lonely, you're way off. What could be better than a girl who's thirty-and-dirty making you feel twenty-with-plenty when you're fifty and shifty? It don't grow on trees and they don't have it at Walmart. So where you gotta go is where it is. All you ever have to pay is the asking price.

They got salamis in France that would make you think twice about your personal hygiene. The fridge was full when we got to the house and a cross-eyed housekeeper in an apron greeted us at the door. Iska continued her conversation with the driver as he unloaded our cases. I began to wonder if she was suddenly becoming a woman without my having noticed. If so, it was another episode in her life when she was anything but 'a little slow.'

It struck me that, apart from her notes, I had little communication with my daughter. I didn't even know who her favorite actor was, or whether she still ate cheeseburgers. That shows you how little I really knew about her life. Pearl smiled at me over coffee in the kitchen, while Billy disappeared and Iska chatted away merrily in French to the housekeeper,

"Dad, her name is Olivia," Iska enlightened me.

Pearl spoke her first words of kindness to me in years, as Iska and the housekeeper appeared through the window in the courtyard, beside some old rusted machine which looked like a giant mangle.

"I think this could be a good holiday, George. Thanks for agreeing to come."

I was touched by her warmth and I knew that this was a moment to savor, as it might provide some encouragement for her not to divorce me if I responded appropriately.

"Don't mention it, Pearl. You know, I think it might be a good time for us here in this house, as a family."

Her eyes lit up and she smiled again just as the silence was broken by Norma-fucking-Desmond.

"Family? What would you know about family? Your son is a cocaine addict, your daughter hardly knows you, and your wife wants a divorce. Family? Don't make me laugh."

"George and I are having a private conversation, Mom. Can you leave us alone for a few minutes?"

I don't think I'd ever heard Pearl give her mother even the whisper of a rebuke before that.

"I know when I'm not wanted," Muriel said, turning her head and marching towards the front of the house. She paused at the door and turned round, smirking, and said, "Heard from your little tramp Goldilocks since you arrived, George?"

"It's Gloria," I snapped back before I'd had a chance to think. Pearl's eyes filled with hurt and she retreated from where she'd been moments earlier.

"Glory be to Gloria," Muriel said, as she left the room. Oh, Fuck.

"Billy's on top of the roof with his drumsticks," Iska announced, as she poked her head round the door from the courtyard. Pearl looked at me like it was all my fault. Maybe it was. I arose wearily from an ancient chair and made my way out into the sunlight.

"Hurry, Dad. He says he's going to jump."

Now one thing I'll say in Billy's favor is that he is decisive. I know it doesn't tip the balance completely perhaps, when weighed against drug addiction and serial stupidity, but it's something. Ever since I can remember, Billy has had at least half a mind of his own. He's threatened to kill other people in the past. He's actually only managed to murder that dog on MV. But, to be fair, this was the first time he'd ever threatened to do away with himself.

The sun beat down on the courtyard and as I got outside I heard the clattery tapping of Billy's drumsticks on the roof tiles. He was clearly not himself, but he was muttering the words to some inane song and it sounded like he was chanting, "Eiderdown any rings tooth decay" and repeating it almost in time to his drumming. He was straddling the top of the roof so only one leg was visible. He was drumming away, shaking his head from side to side in a kind of stupor and, of course, chanting loudly about bedcovers and bad teeth. Oh, and he was naked. The housekeeper was straining to get a glimpse of Billy's slowly bouncing genitalia.

"There's a ladder in the large shed, Dad," Iska said helpfully.

It wasn't readily apparent how Billy had got up there, but that was not my immediate concern. I carried this huge double aluminum ladder out into the sunshine and started to shove it up the wall at the gable end of the house.

"This is all George's fault." Muriel's voice sailed out the kitchen door ahead of her. She was clearly still miles ahead in the bitching stakes because of the kitchen exchange.

"It's nobody's fault, Mom," Pearl countered. "Why do you always have to talk about everything like it was a car accident with you determining liability?"

"Do you think Billy would be sitting on top of the house naked with his drumsticks if his father had managed to remain faithful to you, Pearl?" Muriel moved up a gear and courted a response.

"I don't know, Mom," Pearl answered tiredly.

"Elvis used to shoot light bulbs in his swimming pool," I said jauntily. "Maybe this kind of behavior is just genetic on your side, Muriel?"

"When I lived in Los Angeles, George, marriage was for life." She tossed her head as I pushed the ladder to its fullest extent.

"Tell that to Elizabeth Taylor and Rock Hudson."

"They were not contemporaries of mine." Muriel sucked in warm air and was short of breath for a moment.

"Oh, yes, I forgot. You were a movie star back in the twenties before they invented sound. Ten years earlier and you'd have been a movie star before they invented movies."

"Don't come up here," Billy warned, holding his sticks above his head in a momentary interval in the song. "I'm gonna jump, Dad. I really am."

"It's okay, Billy." I segued into calm-rescuing-parent mode. "I'm only coming up to talk to you." As I spoke, I caught my left foot under a tile which then came loose and slid down the roof, falling thirty feet onto the courtyard where it smashed—unfortunately, some distance from Muriel's head. Pearl and Iska stood together, holding hands and looking up at the sky.

"I mean it, Dad." Billy started to move the one leg I could see back up towards the apex of the roof. I was about fifteen feet from him, and had visions of him standing on the round tile seam at the top and then falling to his demise. I inched forward, using the inside part of my right shoe for a grip against the grainy surface.

"If you want to talk, then talk from there," Billy menaced as best he could.

"I want to talk to you, Billy, about what you are doing." I tried a bit of reason, but I could see by now that his eyes were like blue marbles rolling freely around inside ice cubes.

"What's all this about bedclothes and dentists?" I asked.

"What?" I had his attention.

"You were singing about eiderdowns and tooth decay," I said. "What is that all about, Billy?"

"I was singing the chorus from one of our songs, Dad. 'I disown anything you say, I disown anything you say.' "

"Oh, I thought it was about bedclothes. I thought you said 'eiderdown.' "

"What the fuck is this, Dad? A sudden interest in my lyrics? You're the one who's blocking my career. You won't give your fucking consent to let me follow my dream. What about that? What about that?" He was shouting now and I was getting a pain in my ear, as well as my ass, with the whole scenario.

Over Billy's left shoulder, I could see out beyond the swimming pool and down into the village. There seemed to be a small gathering of people in the square, all shading their eyes and gazing in our direction. On one level I can appreciate that type of attention in a small place where very little happens. But the last thing I wanted for this outdoor Henry family confrontation was an audience.

"I'm gonna jump, Dad." Billy's voice assumed a higher register quality, which probably didn't suit most of his lyrics. All

I could think of was, Jesus, if he jumps forward, maybe he'll kill me as well.

"Billy? Billy!" I really wanted his attention now. He leaned forward and flicked both drumsticks over my head into the courtyard like a true rock star. I contemplated the situation with my eyes level with his nipples.

"Don't come any nearer, I'm fucking warning you, Dad." I was so close to his doped head now that I began to feel a couple of percent Colombian myself.

"I'm not against this rock band thing, Billy. In fact, I'm all for it. You think I really want to stop you from succeeding?"

"You don't even like our music."

"I do," I lied, lyingly.

"Okay then, what's your favorite song?"

" 'Everybody's Got to Learn Sometime' by the Korgis," I replied.

"I mean our songs, the band: East Pole. Do you even know any of our songs?"

I became aware of Pearl waving up at me from just under the eave of the gable end. She had heard Billy's question and was trying to prompt me. I watched as she made gestures indicating whiskers on herself, and then put both of her hands on her head, mimicking ears. The final motion of using her hand as a tail gave me the hint I required.

"The one about cats," I announced. "I like that one."

Billy's face assumed an air of almost reasonableness and he smiled wryly. " 'The Pussy Farm,' you like that song best?"

"Well, I know I never told you before but, yeah, that's the one I like best." (Trust me to choose the fucking stupidest song in their repertoire.)

"But, that's filthy. Grandma says those lyrics are the musical equivalent of Satan's poetry. I can't believe you like that song." He shook his head to emphasize incredulity.

I shook my own head in response. "Well, there you go. Maybe it's the melody which mostly attracts me to it."

If Muriel hated the song, at least that was something in its favor. I had no idea my son was capable of writing lyrics that could piss off the old bitch. Maybe Billy was a genius after all. I couldn't believe Pearl had really meant to prompt that song, though. I mean she's pretty straitlaced.

"Why don't you sing a bit of it, if it's your favorite song by the band?" Billy was emboldened now by this apparent show of knowledge on my part. I knew that it must have been less a desire to have me sing his appalling lyrics on top of a house in France in ninety-degree heat which heartened him at that moment, than a suspicion that I did not know the song and would therefore be exposed as a liar on the first day of our holidays.

"Who am I? The fiddler on the fucking roof, Billy? You sing it and I'll join in, but only if you promise to come down first. Okay?"

"No deal, Dad. You sing the chorus and then I'll come down."

"You're coming down, Billy?" I heard his grandmother's rasping voice interrupt my rescue efforts. "That's great. I knew your dad would sign the contract."

"No, I'm not," he shouted back at her, suddenly remembering that my signature held the key to his dreams. "I'm not coming down until you give your written consent, Dad. Nothing less than that."

The rancid cow, she'd blown any chance of talking him down now and I'd really felt that I was making progress. Time for plan B.

"I've got the contract here," I said, tapping my closed shirt pocket. "I'll sign it now if you want."

"Show me," Billy demanded.

I unbuttoned the pocket and took out the folded document and inched towards him, proffering the paper. Billy leaned forward and took it in his right hand. I figured he'd have to use both hands to unfold it. I was right. He opened the first flap of the paper cautiously and, round about the time he realized it was a list of telephone numbers and e-mail addresses from my office, I punched my only son as hard as I could in the face with my right fist. BANG. Billy dropped the paper and then righted himself with an involuntary movement of his torso, which made him seem still conscious. I waited for the kick or the jump that would signal his intention to kill me, but nothing came. Instead, a gust of wind slapped the paper flat against his chest and, as I had vaguely anticipated with my punch, Billy fell backwards and began to roll down the other side of the roof. I clambered up and grabbed hold of his left ankle as it threatened to disappear from view. I was unable to stop him falling, but I did kinda slow his progress; and in the end his descent from the roof into the kidney-shaped swimming pool was awkward and comical rather than dangerous.

We fished him out pretty much immediately, or rather Iska and Pearl did. He lay panting, coughing up water and occasionally trying to cover his private parts with his hands in odd modest moments of self-conscious lucidity. Wrapped in a towel some minutes later, he announced that he had a headache and wished to lie down. I helped him to his feet and walked him to the downstairs bedroom. Once in bed, I saw him glance quizzically at the bars on the windows and blink to try and refocus. I closed the door behind me, then bolted and padlocked it. There was a vent near the floor through which food and water could be provided if and when required. First up, though, was a double helping of cold turkey.

CHAPTER FOUR

"Hello?" The line crackled as I held the receiver to my ear.

"Hi, can I speak to Billy Henry?" The suave voice on the other end was already on my nerve-endings. I wondered if this might be Billy's dealer.

"Who's this?"

"Who's that?"

"Never mind who's that? Who's this? Tell me or I hang up."

"It's Gooch Witherspoon from Carnivore Records."

"The meat storage company?" I jerked the jerk's chain.

"No, the record company. I'm looking for Billy Henry. I need to speak with him."

"I'm afraid Billy's not available right now."

"Do you know when he'll be back?"

"About 2047," I almost replied, but instead said: "Well, he's got some meeting in Paris tomorrow."

"Who's he meeting? Is it another record company?" Old Gooch was toilet-skid material at this point, so I hooshed his confidence along.

"I don't know, but it's down here in the diary. A girl called Emmy or something."

"Oh, okay, so he's meeting friends, right?" The relief hustled its way down the phone at me for a moment.

"Yes, I guess so. Emmy London her name is, like the city I guess. I'll spell her first name E-M-I."

"E.M.I. London? Jesus!"

"Do you know her?" I smiled but he couldn't tell that through his ear.

"No, no I don't. Just. Well. I wonder if you could get him to call me as soon as he gets back. Could you do that?"

"Sure," I said. "Gimme your number." (But I had his number already, oh yeah).

As I put down the phone I could hear Billy hammering on the door of his room.

"Let me out of this fucking room, Dad. Do you hear me?" I tried to ignore the screaming and the hammering by going out into the garden, but I did hear him and it broke my heart.

The village itself, Gigondas, is a quiet place where there is generally absolutely nothing to do except eat or sleep. Sure, the mountains provide a picturesque backdrop to the quaint red roofs, and the sun oversees the scene like a benign nurse, blah-di-fucking blah and all that, but once you've seen it, you've seen it, if you know what I mean. I gotta say that it's as pretty as a picture. The tiny winding streets are all peppered with sunshine and shade and, here and there, the gurgling of water fountains sounds like pensioners clearing their throats while waiting in line to get served. Anyone I met in the streets stared at me for a moment, like they'd never seen an untanned lawyer before. But they seemed friendly enough too, despite this morbid curiosity.

After the first four or five days we settled into a non-contentious morning routine; I had breakfast with Iska on the terrace about eight-thirty, and Pearl and Muriel usually came down about nine just as we finished our coffee and croissants. Olivia kept stacking pyramids of those small jars of jam on the table each morning. I kinda liked the strawberry one, but the small pictures on the labels looked so similar I kept choosing the raspberry one, which I hated—so I stopped. Life is too short to have to eat raspberry jam when what you really want is strawberry. Analyze that if you want, but it's just me talking.

"Dad, did you know that in Ireland they've got eleven strains of apple that don't grow anywhere else in the world?"

"No, honey. I didn't know that."

"Well, one day maybe we can go there and see. Just to help me write my book, can we, Dad?"

"Sure, sure we can," I replied. But what I really meant was, "Probably not, isn't there a war on there?"

Iska is the person in the family to whom I feel closest. Sure, she's my daughter. But, beyond that, out in the fucking prairie of life where marriage is a cactus, a daughter is the oasis put there to allow fathers to drink something worthwhile in the heat. Iska never makes demands beyond asking me to sign the renewal slip for her library card. That, and costing a fortune in clothes and telephone bills. I got a bill once for her cell phone that was so high I almost slit my throat with the letter-opener after reading it.

"What did you do to rack this up, phone the speaking clock on the moon and not hang up?" I roared at her.

"I just phoned some friends," she replied calmly.

"Well, next time, why don't you just fly them all to Africa for lunch? It would be cheaper."

Two hours later a fax arrived at the house from an airline company giving a quote for chartering a plane to take sixteen children to Casablanca. I never queried her phone bills again.

I decided that each day after breakfast, I'd take a walk in the village. Part of my motivation, at least, was to avoid having to listen to the drone of Muriel's voice echo through the old house like a chainsaw.

"When Hedy Lamarr finished filming *Experiment Perilous* with George Brent, she threw this huge blow-out in Palm Springs. I was dating Trevor Howard's brother at the time and we just . . .'

Sometimes I wanted to grab the old biddy by the throat and shake her till she shut up. But considering the way things were between Pearl and me, a stroll seemed the more sensible course of action.

Days two and three of the cold turkey were the toughest for me. Hearing Billy screaming his lungs out for more drugs, and promising the fucking earth to anyone who'd help him, cut me in two, but I tried to ignore it and went out for more walks. Right in the middle of the village, up a small lane, was a tiny square with just a fountain and a stone bench. I'd often walk through the main square and up around by the grave-yard. Usually I'd just sit on the stone bench, near an old wash house in the shade, before making my way back for lunch. The fountain attracted me because I've always had this thing about running water. I find the sound of it so relaxing that it nearly puts me to sleep. I'd read the week-old *Herald Tribune* they sold in the small tobacco shop, and get the results of ballgames I'd attended before we left the U.S. The other thing about running water—when you're over fifty—is sometimes the sound makes you have to pee more often than you'd normally be comfort-able with. "Swings and roundabouts," as someone I know in the law business says.

All the thoughts of peeing made me recall the findings of an autopsy, which was read into the record at an inquest I attended in my first week as a qualified lawyer (twenty-five years ago). The deceased had been shot in a fight over a parking space in an underground garage beneath a department store. The victim had pulled a knife to make his point, but the rival for the car space had a Magnum 45 and blew the knife-thrower's face off. Anyway, the thing is, I attended the inquest on behalf of the owners of the garage. They were afraid of being sued for not making the spaces small enough so that both parties could have had a parking space each! (Don't believe me? See Commonwealth of Mass. v. Gardner, 1976.) When the autopsy report was read into the record it contained the phrase, "penis and testicles unre-markable." Talk about kicking someone in the nuts when they can't fight back. So it made me wonder one day at the foun-tain whether my own equipment would be deemed "unremark-able" when I died. I suppose the alternative verdicts would be, "noteworthy" or maybe even—in exceptional circumstances— "impressive" or "Oh, my God!" (See what paranoia one is cursed with when spare time and middle age intersect?)

"Billy's been sick again," Pearl said, when I got back for lunch on the Thursday after we'd arrived. This was day five of the cold turkey.

"He'll be fine," I responded, sitting down in an armchair in the front room from where I could see Muriel and Iska in bathing suits on their way around the corner to the pool.

"I mean really sick, George. Mom says he's been coughing blood and asked her to call a doctor."

"He's faking it, Pearl. Drugs make liars out of ordinary people."

"Billy's not just an ordinary person, George. He's our son." She picked up a magazine from the coffee table and threw it back down. It had Saddam Hussein on the cover with half his head stained by espresso.

"Look, Pearl. I know things haven't been easy, but just trust me on this, okay? This is the best thing for Billy right now."

"Trust you because you're a lawyer?" Pearl half-smiled, recalling a standing joke between us.

"Something like that." I smiled back.

Screams brought us running from the front room. Billy was yelling like a madman inside the door as we arrived.

"She's an animal. The fucking bitch, she's an animal."

As Olivia pushed a tray of food through the flap, Billy had grabbed her hand and tried to break her wrist.

"I am sorry, Mr. and Mrs. Henry, he grabbed my hand, so I bit his finger." Iska dripped water onto the stone flag floor as she interpreted the housekeeper's apology. Billy kept slamming at the door with his fists and demanding to be let out. Muriel stood accusingly in the kitchen with her hands on her hips and her sagging skin falling around her like melting ice cream. Here and there, the hint of tan peeked out between the folds. Even though her expression said it all, she felt compelled to augment that statement with the use of her vocal cords.

"This is all your fault, George Baxter Henry. Pearl should never have married you. I was against it from the start." She folded her arms in a defiant full-stop to this disclosure.

"I wasn't a million percent in favor of it myself," I said. "A mixture of ignorance and good faith made me think that by marrying Pearl I'd rescue her from you and a lifetime of Clark-fucking-Gable anecdotes. Plus, I'd fallen in love with her and thought that any obstacles you could put in our way would be surmountable with a cocktail of affection and wishful thinking."

"You've never thought about anyone but yourself, George," Muriel responded. "If you thought you'd get away with it, you'd sell your own children if there was a profit in it. Look at you, fifty-something with a cocaine addict for a son and a two-week counseling course for a marriage. Even Iska doesn't understand what's going on around her. Maybe if she knew you were humping some slut on the ninth floor instead of caring for her mother, things would be clearer for her."

"Leave Iska out of this, Mom," Pearl intervened. "My marital problems are my own business, not yours or Iska's."

"If you'd listened to me all those years ago, you'd have married somebody suitable instead of scraping the barrel for an engagement ring and a time-share in George's pecker."

"Suitable? Like who?" Pearl said heatedly. "Like that bald pervert whose father made his fortune in pool-cleaning solutions? Or maybe the lazy son of some film star who could drink champagne all day, then come home every night and punch my lights out?"

"Like someone who had a little class, Pearl. Your mother was a famous actress. She was respected and adored. What possessed you to marry the son of an olive-oil salesman? Your mother did everything she could to give you opportunities, and all you could do was throw them back in her face! How dare you!"

"Grandma? Grandma?" Billy's voice rang out plaintively from the other side of the door. We all stopped to listen.

"Yes, Billy dear?" Muriel pulled a towel around her shoulders like a cape, and shrugged to emphasize that she was the only one capable of eliciting sensible talk from Billy.

"Stop talking about yourself in the third person! And what's with the past tense thing? It makes you sound like you're dead. You'll only get Dad's hopes up," Billy said. There was a maniacal snigger after this from him and then complete silence. Iska started to laugh and even Pearl grinned a little. Muriel turned on her bare heels and went back out to the pool.

I don't want to go into too much detail about the attempt to detox Billy but, suffice to say, it's a good thing the room had a bathroom attached to it. The only things within the reach of my junkie son were: a mattress, a toilet bowl, toilet paper, a faucet and a basin. In almost a week now he hadn't even eaten, but he had been able to drink plenty of water and shit the stuff out of his system. Someone once told me that the Italian for suppository is innuendo. Suicide is the biggest risk to people in cold turkey, as far as I've read. Billy had no belt, no shoelaces, and nothing to stand on or hang from. The need for all of this had been clearly spelled out to the realtor when we booked the place. At home in Boston this kind of treatment would have been much more difficult to organize—with dealers and fellow coke-heads only a local call away. I know that there was nothing scientific about the method I'd chosen to clear Billy's system, but it was the best I could come up with. I have to confess that, apart from a few discreet enquiries to Karl, a former psychiatric nurse who now sells newspapers, the treatment was pretty much my own recipe.

"Just don't leave him anything he could hang himself with," Karl had said.

"What about medication to ease him off the stuff?" I'd asked innocently.

"You'll need the medication, George. Just keep the door locked and your ears closed."

We could have gotten Billy into the Betty Ford Clinic, but who wants to spend two hundred thousand dollars to find out that their son is incurable? Not me. Not even Dr. Volt's suggestion about detox marshals appealed to me for even a second. Sometimes you gotta do the parenting yourself. I looked in at

Billy that night, and he was asleep like a baby on the mattress with a plastic cup of water on the floor beside him. If things didn't get any worse, maybe they'd get better.

Let me say that what I really wanted to happen at that time was for Billy to get better and for Pearl not to divorce me. I also wanted good things for Iska and, of course, bad things for Muriel. That was about the height of it in early August 1999 in Gigondas, that cute village which survived quite well despite the absence of fast food outlets or an organized sex industry.

One day early on in the "holiday," maybe on a Monday or something, I saw a group of four or five men, mostly in their seventies I guessed, playing a game in the shade of some trees in the main square. The trees were old and sort of grey, with huge warts on their trunks looking like some branches that had never got going. The tops of the trees were an awkward shape as they spread out in thick short branches with clumps of leaves at the end of each. The men each had a set of three metal balls like slightly reduced baseballs. The trick seemed to be to get closest to a small wooden ball they threw ten or fifteen yards ahead before each game. The terrain was sandy gravel, and the trees threw enough shade to allow them to play without being oppressed by the heat. I watched them that day and was mesmerized by the calm which seemed to shroud their competition. The oldest of them appeared the best player: a man in a blue suit with a white tie and a flat cap. After that first morning, I sought them out each day and, you know, the one time they weren't there I felt sad. They spoke to each other in low voices, and from time to time looked over at me and then back at each other and spoke again. On the first few occasions, they'd barely acknowledged my presence as I watched them. But, over a week or so, they gradually came to nod hello in my direction when I came into view around the corner. In the afternoon, sometimes, I saw them gathered at a table outside the small hotel in the square, drinking Pernod, reviving their drinks with water which made the glasses cloudy.

One day as I entered the phone booth, one of them raised his glass to me in a salute. I put coins in the slot and dialed.

"Hello?"

"Hi, is this Gloria?"

"Yeah, who's this?"

"George."

"George?" The voice became muffled as though she'd put her hand over the receiver.

"Hello, Gloria? Are you still there?"

"Sure, sure. Where are you, George? Are you back in Boston?"

"No, I'm still in France, we're in this small village. It's very hot."

"I'm very hot too, George," she said slowly. I could picture her there in her short skirt with her tits pushed high and frontal in some tight t-shirt.

"I got your message on my answering machine last night, but I couldn't call you from the house because of—"

"I know, I know, your wife Priscilla."

"Pearl," I corrected.

"Oh yeah, Pearl. I forgot, Priscilla is someone else."

"Elvis's wife."

"Who?"

"Elvis Presley's wife was called Priscilla."

"You know Priscilla Presley? George you're amazing." I didn't even reply to try and sort that one out. I saw the fucking telephone meter thing flashing, so I put in a few more coins.

"What's up, Gloria? You sounded concerned on the answering machine."

"Yeah, George. I know you said I was only to call in an emergency, but this is an emergency."

My heart leaped into my fucking mouth and started to bounce my face all over the phone booth. Pregnant. It had to be.

"Okay," I said calmly. "Tell me what's wrong." I closed my eyes and awaited the inevitable.

"I need a new car, George."

"What? You need a new car? You fucking telephone me to where I'm not, when I'm away, to have me call you from five hours ahead just to tell me that?"

"Don't get mad, George."

"Oh, I'm not mad," I shouted. "I'm absolutely fucking livid."

"George, George," she calmed me from five-and-a-half-thousand miles. "Listen."

"Yes?"

"Do you love me, George?"

"What?" I couldn't believe this shit.

"Do-you-love-me-George?"

"Of course I do, of course I do. Why do you think I bang you every Wednesday and pay your credit card? Out of animosity, is that what you think?"

"Oh, George, I don't know. You're miles away and I need to be with you. Maybe if you could buy me a new car, I could drive to see you in France."

"James fucking Bond couldn't drive from Boston to France," I said. I heard something, or someone, as she started sobbing, like as if it was someone saying, "Don't worry, Baby."

"Are you alone, Gloria?"

"Of course. Why are you asking that, George?"

"I thought I heard someone there with you."

"No, no, of course not, George. It's eight o'clock in the morning." A door slammed somewhere behind her.

"What the fuck was that?"

"The plumber," she said. "He was just looking at my boiler." Her tone of voice is worried now. I decide not to lay it on too thickly.

"A plumber, at eight in the morning?"

"He was just passing by and remembered I'd called him out about a week ago."

"Just passing by? In what? A fucking helicopter? You live on the seventeenth floor."

"Are you going to divorce her, George? I need some stability in my life." She sobbed on the phone as time clicked away.

"Divorce? You know, we're talking about that, Gloria. We're actually talking about that at the moment. But it's difficult to find time to discuss it properly what with Billy and all. Look, I'm out of coins here."

"What about the new car?" She sounded remarkably coherent and sob-free now.

"I'll sort out the limit on the card, okay? Try Chaney Philips down at Faneuil, he's got those new Mazdas. Okay?"

"Okay, George. Bye, take care, I'll be—" The coins ran out. I got some more change in the hotel and rang my secretary.

"Yes, Mr. Henry? How are things in France?"

"Pretty good, Judy," I lied. "Any calls since yesterday?"

"That Mr. Witherspoon called and asked me for your address. He says your number in France is always busy."

"It's off the hook. Don't give him the address."

"Okay. Anything else I can do?"

"Yes, Judy. You know that credit card I got for that lady in Global Translating?"

"Yes?"

"Call the bank and talk to Arnie Bollster. Tell him to change the limit to fifty."

"Fifty thousand?"

"No, fifty bucks. Old Gloria has found another sponsor from what I can tell. Some plumber's looking at her pipes."

"Hot and cold, Mr. Henry?" she said, as she laughed.

"Absol-fucking-lutely, Judy." Click. I don't mind infidelity, but I won't tolerate breach of contract.

Back in the house, I heard voices. Iska was sitting on the floor outside Billy's room, reading to him.

"In Devonshire, that's in England, they used to do this thing on Twelfth Night back in the 1800's. It was called wassailing and it means thanking the God of Apples so they'd get good cider that year. Should I keep reading?" There was silence from the drug tank. "Okay, Billy, I'm going to stop now if you're tired of hearing me read." Iska closed the book with a slam, but I saw she'd marked the page.

"Don't go, Iska. Tell me more about the goddamn apples," Billy said. I could hear my own voice in my son's. Iska looked up at me and winked as I passed by her. I kissed my index finger and hunched down to transfer the kiss to the tip of her nose.

Night eight in the cell and Billy's asked for some milk and cookies. No meat yet, but maybe Carnivore's dream is gonna come true.

CHAPTER FIVE

"The Clever Boy is tall and young,
Well educated; speaks many tongues
The Clever Girl stays a step ahead;
She does all her sleeping in her own bed.
Drink yourself insensible, life has passed you by
Miss Galore says she wants more; but you can't even try.

(and then the chorus)
You can come, you can come, but you'll come
　　to no harm; down on the Pussy Farm.
(repeat chorus)."

I'd gone through Billy's suitcase, looking for clean clothes
to throw under the door to him, and a folder full of lyrics
had tumbled out. Some of the titles were of the predictable
suicidal-teenager variety like that nut Kurt Cockburn wrote
(from whatever the band was called, Valhalla or something).
Of course, I was curious to find the words to the song I'd pretended to like up on the roof two weeks earlier. To be honest,
I was impressed at the kid's ability not only to string sentences
together, but to rhyme them too. Despite the subject matter,
I was pretty proud of old Billy. Not only the lyrics, but the
coke thing as well; he was now eleven days without the stuff
and eating almost normally. He was still in the room, but a

letter had arrived for him so I'd opened it and read it to him through the door.

"They want you in New York on the sixteenth to start recording, Billy."

"That's in five days' time, Dad."

"I can count."

"So what's gonna happen, Dad?"

"About what?" (As if I didn't know.)

"About the contract? The band? Are you going to give your consent or what?"

"We said four weeks of clean urine samples, Billy. Remember?"

"That was two weeks ago, Dad."

"Eleven days ago, Billy, a week and a half."

"So I'm clean eleven days. That's not bad."

"Eleven days in a room in France with a reinforced door and bars on the windows, I'd hardly call it, 'voluntary detox.'"

"It's a start, Dad. It's a start. So, I needed a helping hand. And I'm eating."

"You were eating a week ago, Billy. Only it was the house-keeper's hand you wanted for lunch."

"I'm sorry 'bout that, Dad."

"I know, Billy, so is she."

There was silence. I took the key out of my pocket and opened the door. Billy stood in the middle of the room wearing a Bart Simpson t-shirt and khaki shorts. His feet were bare and the stink from the bathroom brought me back to my diaper-changing days.

"You wanna come out, Billy?"

"Sure, Dad." He began to walk towards me.

"Here's the deal, Billy," I said. "You stay clean until the night of the fifteenth and I'll put you on the plane with the contract signed."

"And after that?"

"After that you're on your own, Billy, you can do what you like with whatever it is you got coming."

"You mean that, Dad?" He was incredulous.

"Sure. We all gotta make our own way, Billy, and you're old enough to make up your own mind about things. We all gotta cut loose someday and make our own mistakes."

"That's it, Dad? Stay clean for five days and I'm home free?" His eyes were brighter now than they'd been in months.

"Yep. Just one small thing."

"Name it."

I produced a bound deed and handed it to him. He walked to the kitchen reading it. Once there, he sat at the table and flipped over to the second page. His eyes widened as he read down to the end.

"A million dollars? I have to pay you a million dollars?"

"Read the conditions, Billy. Only if you test positive for any illegal substances in blood or urine in the next five years. I can turn up anywhere, any when, with a doctor, and you consent to giving him a blood or urine sample."

"And in return for this?"

"In return, you get my signature, along with your mom's, to let you get on the plane in five days' time."

"And I have to give a blood sample to the local doctor before we leave for the airport?"

"You got it. Take it or leave it, Billy."

"How much time have I got to consider this proposal?"

"All the time you need, say, by three this afternoon." (It was two-thirty now.)

"What about independent legal advice?"

"You're lookin' at it." I grinned.

"So what's your independent legal advice then, Dad?"

"Don't sign, you're not mentally up to keeping your part of the bargain."

"You're telling me not to sign, and yet at the same time you're the person who drafted the agreement for me to sign in the first place! What's that about?"

"Can't get more independent than that, Billy."

"Suppose I can't pay you the million bucks, what happens then?"

"Then you'll have to file for bankruptcy, which you'll see, from the new contract Carnivore sent, allows them to treat your contract as being at an end, and to terminate it with a declaration that you owe them two million for breach of clause 11.4."

"So it's win-win for everyone except me?" Billy smiled.

"You got it, Billy. What's it gonna be?"

"Gimme that pen, Dad."

By the time Billy got around to getting legal advice on the enforceability of our deal, he would either be on his way to crack-cocaine heaven or so clean or rich he wouldn't give a fuck either way. I folded the deed and pocketed it.

"What's the pool like, Dad?" Billy began to take off his t-shirt.

"Don't you remember? No, of course not, last time you swam there you were asleep."

Making Carnivore nervous about a rival company's interest had really paid dividends. Their new contract offered twice the money the first one had, and the royalties from Billy's lyrics would no longer be carrying the financial can if the album flopped. Cross-collateralization, my swizzle stick!

"Would you like to play, Monsieur?" It was almost the end of our second week in France and the ice was finally broken with the old guys and their game of boules. One of them offered me a spare set of metal balls.

"Sure," I said, shifting my ass off the wall and walking over to where the three old guys stood in the long shadow cast by a plane tree. (That's what the guidebook calls them.) One of the regulars hadn't turned up and I got my big chance.

"American?" one of the other two asked. I nodded and shrugged my shoulders in a gesture I hoped would disarm them of their prejudice.

"John Wayne, George Bush, Jane Fonda." The third guy smiled as he intoned the names of our national heroes.

"Charles de Gaulle, Cézanne, Pinochet." I did my best to reciprocate. All three men laughed, and one after another extended their hands and introduced themselves.

"De Gaulle."

"Cézanne."

"Pinochet," the expert with the white tie said. "And you?"

"George," I replied.

They all cracked up laughing and one of them said, "Mesteer Bush," and we were off.

We played in pairs and I was fucking awful for the first few games, but got the hang of it near lunchtime. We adjourned for a drink and, as I finished mine, I made a knife and fork gesture and pretended to gobble food. They understood.

"Tomorrow?" The oldest guy made throwing signs with his hand curled towards him, indicating play.

"Oui, oui," I said, using the only French word I knew.

On the way back to the house, I took a different route and passed by an old schoolhouse. There was a war memorial on the roadside nearby. I read down through the list and my eye was caught by a name which seemed familiar: "Eugene Aragon." I knew what it was that made me look twice. Some of the old wine bottles in the kitchen over the cooker had candles in them, and the name "Aragon" appeared on the labels. I don't know if there was a connection between the house and this guy Eugene; but anyhow it sorta surprised me that I noticed something that was French and had at least made the connection in my mind, if you know what I mean. The twenty-fifth of February 1916 was the day he'd died. I'd never really thought about the First World War much, because nobody I knew had been caught up in it. My old man had been in the next one, though. There was a photograph, somewhere at home, of him in his uniform with one of his comrades lying on a sand dune in Normandy with the sun in his eyes.

I traced some of the names on the memorial with a finger and became aware of someone watching me. I looked around, and this gorgeous broad was standing with a bicycle on the other side of the road. Her bicycle faced towards the village, but she was pointed the other way, staring back up the road in my direction. At first I thought that perhaps she was related to someone listed on the memorial, and was concerned that a stranger was poking at their name with a foreign finger. She didn't seem unhappy, though. She was very pretty, with long legs which were nearly up to her ears. She wore a sky blue blouse with the sleeves rolled up her arms, like she was ready for some hard work. Her skirt was a sort of apron, all white and tied around her waist like a hug.

We stared at each other for a few moments, then she asked, in pretty good English.

"You are staying at the Montmirail house?" She pointed towards our holiday home.

"Yes," I answered, somewhat short of breath because of the effect she was having on my "unremarkable" equipment beneath the shallow cover of my cotton slacks. I wondered if my excitement was visible to her. She seemed to give me a once-over before hopping on her bicycle and freewheeling the short trip down to the village square. She was some honey bunch, I don't mind telling you. Old Gloria Dinerman wouldn't be fit to unclip her bra (I'd reserve that onerous task for myself). Being a non-trial lawyer, it had to have been a while since I'd filed an affidavit, but I wouldn't have minded filing one in her court-room office. What a bitch Gloria was, trying to pull the fast one on me when I was thousands of miles away, rebuilding my marriage. Jesus, she had some nerve, I thought, as I watched one of the cutest asses I'd ever seen, freewheel out of view.

Iska had found a new strain of Peruvian apple on the internet and she told me all about it at breakfast. "You know, Dad, they tie glass jars on the buds with a string and the apples grow square. Can you believe that?"

"Unbelievable," I said, with my mouth full of croissant and strawberry (no, fuck, raspberry) jam. God, I hate raspberries. Iska seemed in pretty good form.

"Billy's talking to Hairy and Joe by e-mail, Dad. They're so excited about recording the single next week. Hairy says that they've got this producer lined up who worked with Eye Twitch and Stainmaster."

"Wow!" I tried to sound impressed.

"I think it's all noise," Muriel said, sneaking up behind me and grabbing the pot of coffee. "When I made movies, they used orchestras. They had to play live, too, when they recorded the music. Now it's all computers and electric bells."

"I think Billy's a good lyricist," I pitched in.

"A good lyricist? Are you out of your mind, George? Billy is a very sick boy who writes evil lyrics. He's a Satanist at heart."

"At least he has a heart, Muriel." I came to Billy's defense. "I understand you were scheduled for a heart transplant once, but they couldn't find enough granite."

Pearl came out onto the veranda in her dressing gown. For the first time, I noticed that she'd lost a little weight and looked tanned.

"Your husband is being his usual nasty snide self," Muriel addressed Pearl.

"I'm sure you're well able to handle it, Mom." Pearl flicked her lack of concern at her mother with a glance and a sway of her hips as she came round to my side of the table and sat in a deck chair near me.

"Billy's doing really well, George," Pearl said, as she put her rolled-up towel on her lap and leaned in to pour herself some coffee.

"He's still got a long way to go, Pearl," I warned.

"Yeah, Billy's gonna be a superstar," Iska laughed, clapping her hands together. "He's gonna be a millionaire."

"It'd be great to have a real superstar in the family," I said, biting into a dry piece of bread, hoping it would counteract the taste of raspberries. I could feel Muriel's eyes boring into the top of my head as I looked down at the rolled-up towel and imagined Pearl unraveling it at the edge of the pool and then lying on it and . . .

"I was a star of the silver screen." Muriel interrupted my coarse thoughts about her daughter.

"Oh, yeah, I forgot," I said, grinning. "*Turn Right at the Golden Gate Bridge.*"

"*Turn Left at the Brooklyn Bridge*," she corrected. "You know the name of the film I got my nomination for, George. Don't try and pretend you don't. I caught you watching it six months ago on a rental video. So don't deny it."

"Of course, I don't deny it, Muriel. But I have to confess I watched it with ulterior motives."

"Ulterior motives?" She seemed surprised.

"Yeah," I said casually. "I wanted to see if there were any other elements in the film, besides your own Oscar-nominated performance, which would explain its complete commercial failure."

"Art is not about money, George. Of course, I wouldn't expect a soulless commercial lawyer to understand that."

"Why do you two have to argue all the time?" Iska intervened, looking up from her square apples printout.

"Because your grandmother is a former silent screen star who just can't shut the fuck up." I tried 'owning' my feelings out loud.

"George!" Pearl snapped. "Not in front of the children, please. I don't want that kind of language in this family."

"Or that kind of husband." Muriel threw a final punch.

"Tell us about Clark Gable and Humphrey Bogart." Iska invited her grandmother to press the 'rewind' and 'play' buttons simultaneously.

"Well, honey. It was the week after Carole Lombard and I had returned from vacation in Miami. We had just started shooting *Mr. and Mrs. Smith* and then . . ."

I wandered off to try and find some paint drying I could watch instead.

Billy was out in the courtyard behind the house. He was wearing his discman while drumming along on an old wine cask that looked even more tired than I felt. I stood at a distance watching him with his eyes closed and his drumsticks tapping rhythm on wood that was probably a hundred years old. I'd seen him do this before at home, when I'd stopped him from using the full drum kit in the basement to allow the neighborhood a couple of hours sleep. As I watched, I tried to remember what Billy had been like as a child and the times we'd had together. But, you know, when I thought back, it seemed like I was always either shouting at him or he was beheading neighbors' pets.

"The Happy Boy treats his lady right;
Up on time and stays up all night.
The Happy Girl cannot be denied;
Purrs like a—"

"What, Dad? Did you say something?" Billy unplugged his earpieces and switched off the discman.

"I was just recalling the lyrics of one of your songs."

"One of our songs? You mean East Pole?"

"Yeah."

"Which one?"

"The one about the cats, 'The Pussy Farm.'" I felt myself blush for the first time in about thirty years.

"Go on then, let's hear it, Dad." Billy stood opposite me and, for the first time ever, I noticed he was taller than me.

"The Happy Girl cannot be denied," I recited. Billy joined in,
"Purrs like a kitten when she's satisfied.
Call me a perfectionist; it's just the way I am.
No more six feet tall with one inch small, I need
a man."

We finished verse two and laughed together like a pair of drains for the first time since God knows when.

A few days later, I was on my morning walk when I did a double take. I retraced a couple of paces and saw a scene I'd never imagined having to deal with. Iska was sitting on the steps of a narrow tall house holding hands with a tanned boy who seemed about the same age. As I watched, they kissed lightly and looked into each other's eyes. She didn't notice me, and I doubt that she would have even if I'd been standing between them. My instinct as a father was, of course, to skewer the little French runt with a flagpole and beat him to a pulp for taking advantage of my daughter. But I didn't. They both seemed to be equally culpable. Who the fuck was I to stomp on her dreams? She's the only one in the family who really keeps me sane.

The first time I ever kissed a girl, it was this pig-tailed broad called Julie Miller. I remember it was on the corner of the street where she lived. I chanced a kiss outta view of her house; only her dad was passing by in his rusty Buick and he got out and told Julie to get into the car. Then he smacked me so hard in the teeth I nearly landed in next year's school photograph. Ah, memories, memories . . .

I continued my walk and made a detour from my normal route, and arrived out onto a small track above the village that leads up into the mountains. Half a mile up the track turns right, and on the left is an old ruined cottage in the shadow of a clump of cypress trees. From there, a wonderful view of the village is the reward for the trek. It's like a small oasis in the desert. The houses huddle down around the square and the sun drops by for company. Jeez, I'm beginning to sound like a fucking tourist brochure. I sat for a while in the shade of a tree and the sun fell all around me like a blanket. The humidity was something else, and ultimately the only way to get any relief was to take off my shirt and fan myself with it. I kept thinking about that girl on the bicycle near the war memorial, and the recollection of her raised much more than a tremor. I could tell you about how I managed with great self-restraint to ignore my unexpected erection, but I'd be lying. Invigorated by my morning jaunt, I jogged back down the track and paddled in a stream above the graveyard, before joining Pinochet and the others for our daily game.

> "Spend your days just watching and your nights
> just learning how;
> Doggie does it from behind. Pussy says 'Meow . . .'"

It was less than twenty-four hours before the flight to New York when I got Olivia to phone the local doctor to come and test Billy. After six days of recording, East Pole would have a day full of press interviews and then Billy would fly back to join us for the last two weeks of our holiday. The album would be completed in September. True to their word, the record company wired two hundred and fifty thousand dollars into my account in trust for Billy. It was an advance against lyric royalties for the music publishing end of things. I honestly couldn't fucking believe it, but I tried hard to.

That night, there was a knock on the partition door. I slid the bolt back and Pearl was there in her dressing gown, wearing the red underwear I'd gotten her in Vegas three years earlier.

"Can I come in, George?"

"Sure, honey." We got into bed together for the first time in months.

"I'm so proud of the way you dealt with Billy," she whispered, snuggling up so close to me that I could smell the toothpaste on her breath.

"Trust me, I'm a lawyer," I said, as her hand found the back of my neck and pulled me in for a kiss.

> "You can come, you can come, but you'll come
>   to no harm . . ."
> (Repeat chorus)

CHAPTER SIX

"I hope you're not back sleeping with him, Pearl."

Muriel's voice was clear as a bell through the open window of the landing on the first floor. I was sitting on the window seat, out of the heat of the Provençal sun, reading. Pearl and Muriel were lying on sun beds beside the pool.

"Of course not, Mom. It's far too early into this whole process for anything like that."

"I knew it, I knew it. You are sleeping with him, aren't you?"

"I told you, Mom, I'm not."

"I don't believe you. I always know when you're fibbing, Pearl. Remember the time you let that Landers boy see your tootie? I knew you were fibbing then."

"For Christ's sake, Mom, that was forty years ago. I was ten."

"So you are back sleeping with George?"

"Mom, let it go please."

"You've got to divorce him, Pearl. There's no other way. He's worth more to you in a divorce settlement than he is dead. You get sixty percent of his share of the law firm and alimony and child support. When I struck that deal for you there were three other partners. Now there's only George and Ivel Schwartz. How much is that gonna be? Three, four, five million, ten million? He'll have to borrow if he wants to stop the firm from being liquidated. Maybe Ivel would buy him out?"

"Mom," Pearl shrieked, "I-do-not-want-a-divorce."

"Then you want your head examined. Look, I told you before we even came here, all you have to do is keep away from him for six weeks. Then file for divorce and say you tried reconciliation, but it didn't work. A couple of well-placed sobs in court, plus the photographs of George's ass in the air while he's giving Gloria some, and who knows, you might even take him for seventy-five percent of everything."

"Mom, will you please shut up. George and I will work our way through this. I know he's going to change. It's a midlife crisis and we'll get past it. Okay? So just butt out."

"You want to be worrying about who he's with or what he's doing when you're my age, huh? Is that what you want? Get out now and take him for as much as you can. That's my advice."

"I don't want to grow old alone, Mom," Pearl said.

"You mean like me? Is that what you mean? Your father and I were faithful to each other. Don't you think you could find someone else who would be faithful if you had all that money?"

"You mean pay someone to be my husband?"

"Don't be ridiculous, Pearl. You know what I mean."

"No, I don't."

"Live a little, Pearl. You deserve a second chance. George is not going to suddenly change his spots and only want to sleep in his wife's bed."

"He hasn't been there for a long time, Mom. Maybe I haven't been paying him enough attention. Maybe that's why he went somewhere else."

I could sense from her voice that Pearl was close to tears.

"He went somewhere else because he's a rat, Pearl. He has serial middle-age infidelity. It's a condition brought on by a combination of the presence of younger women and the absence of prostate cancer. Face it, Pearl, you've got to get rid of him. Find someone else if you're afraid of being lonely."

"I don't want anyone else, Mom. That's why I married him. Now this conversation is at an end or I'm going swimming."

"All I'm saying is . . ."

SPLASH.

In actual fact, Pearl wasn't lying when she'd said she wasn't back sleeping with me. When she'd come into my room the previous night we'd had a couple of preliminary smooches and gropes, only Pearl had pulled back from any further intimacy just as I had been all fired up and ready to go.

"I can't, George. I'm sorry." She rolled away from me and began to get out of bed.

"What? What is it, Pearl? Are you ill or something?" (I'd tactfully avoided the phrase 'time of the month' because to the best of my recollection that particular ailment had abandoned Pearl in the 1980's.)

"No, George, I'm not ill." She stood up. "It's just that it's too soon, that's all."

"Too soon? We've been here two weeks, for God's sake."

"I don't mean that, George. I mean it's too soon after the shock of your . . ." She searched for the word. "Your connection with that woman."

"My, 'connection'?"

"Yes, George. It's too soon after that. I need time to let my feelings readjust to the man you've become."

"What do you mean? You think I've changed, that I'm not the same old George you've always known?"

"No, George, you're not. You've slept with someone else and I need time to come to terms with that. I thought I would be ready now for, well—you know. But I'm not. I'm sorry, George, but I need some more time."

She kissed me on the lips as a sort of disallowed appetizer and then went back to her own room. This divorce thing might be harder to head off at the pass than I'd thought. The conversation I'd overheard, however, led me to believe that Pearl was genuine in her efforts to save our marriage, but I really had to be wary of Muriel's influence. Why didn't the old cow just up and die? I'd have poisoned her; only you just can't buy hemlock in that kind of quantity without a license.

The thing about the deal that Muriel had brokered was that, if we divorced, then the law firm would be liquidated and the partnership dissolved. Sixty percent of my net worth at that point was somewhere in the region of seven million dollars, as the partnership had acquired quite a bit of real estate along the way. We were a commercial law firm and I could expect to treble or quadruple my stake between now and sixty-five, if things continued at the same pace. Even borrowing that kind of money in a divorce scenario, to avoid losing the firm, would be cripplingly hard to do. If that happened, the repayments would catch up with me before the Green Reaper did. No, it was clear to me what had to be done: my marriage had to be saved at all costs. Muriel was absolutely correct in her assessment of Pearl's bargaining power in a divorce court. The lethal combination of my infidelity and Pearl's vulnerability might result in even bigger damages than I was reckoning on. I had to face up to my responsibilities as a husband and a father. Marriage is always cheaper in the long run. A couple of months of lawyers' letters and a two-day hearing, with Muriel and the P.I. swearing up, would ruin me. I might still be able to retire to the Bahamas, but I'd be mixing the cocktails myself and that wasn't what I wanted.

"What's the weather like in New York?" I asked Billy when he phoned a few days later.

"Hot as Hell, Dad, but we're really enjoying the studio. You'll never guess who dropped in to see us yesterday and just hang out?"

"Who?"

"E.L.B.L., the rapper from Iowa."

"Wow-ee, that's fantastic, Billy." (I had no idea who the fuck this BLT guy was, but whatever.)

"Looks like your favorite song's gonna be the single, Dad." Billy's voice echoed across the Atlantic.

"The one about the cats?"

"That's the one, Dad."

"So are you on a break now or what, Billy?"

"Yeah, we've got the afternoon off and then it's back to the grind till Friday when the publicity begins. *Rolling Stone* is sending a photographer over and we're gonna do the shots for the album cover, too. Looks like we'll have half the songs in the can by then."

"You're still coming back to join us for the last two weeks?"

"Sure am. I can't wait to take you all out to dinner and spend some of this dough."

"I talked to Ivel and he's got some good ideas about investments. You should think about buying a house, bricks and—"

"Bricks and mortar. I know, I know. When we all get back to Boston, I'm gonna organize a trip for the whole lot of us, to guess where?"

"The moon? Who am I, the fucking memory man?"

"Memphis, Dad. To see the spiritual home of the Henry family." He laughed and so did I.

"Absolutely great, Billy. Grandma will love that," I said, as she passed by me in the hall on her way out. She gave me a look that would have squeezed an all-male Golf Club out of *The Vagina Monologues*.

"I gotta go now, Dad. I'll phone before I get the flight on Tuesday, okay? Just to let you know when I'll be back."

"Okay, Billy."

"Okay, Dad."

"Hey, Billy?" I said, before he hung up.

"Yeah, Dad?"

"You're keeping your nose clean, right?"

He sniffed down the line like a snorting goat. "You hear that, Dad?"

"I hear it."

"Clean as a whistle."

"Okay, Billy, just be good, okay?"

"You got it, Dad." He hung up.

That night I checked the phone messages at the office. There was one call from some jerk in Billy's college in Lansing, asking if I could phone the Alumni Bequests and Donations office before the end of the week, for an urgent message. I guessed it was some prick trying to put the hammer on me for more dough to let Billy pass the September resits in Bolivian hysteria. Fuck them. Billy was on his way to a post-Colombian Ph.D. in success if everything panned out properly for him. I realized that since he'd flown home, I'd found myself relating to him in a completely different way than I had in the previous seventeen years. Billy had talent. Okay, maybe not in departments I'd heard of, but, hey, who knew what might happen? Perhaps he would be a rock star and make tons of bread and last a good few years at the top. Who was I to stop him in his chosen path and make him sidestep my own shortsightedness in order to grab onto his dream? Iska was finding her feet too, so that was another phase to be handled as a father. I didn't want to stand in their way and have silent feuds with them when they were thirty. I wanted to be a part of their lives and, if I could prevent them from overdosing or underachieving, perhaps that's all a fucking parent can do. Maybe the key to hanging on to your kids is knowing when to let go.

"George, please call me. I'm in Carrington Street Precinct station. There's been a terrible mistake." Gloria's panicky sobbing sounded strangely authentic when I checked my phone messages again later the same day. I was delighted that she'd run into some trouble after her brush with the Angel Temerity in letting some plumber turn her taps.

"Mr. Henry, sorry to bother you, but we got a little problem here in Carrington. I wonder if you could call us as soon as you get this message. It's probably nothing, but we got a broad here on a credit card felony who says you promised to pay for a new Mazda even though her card was maxed out. Ask for Sergeant Hanwick."

I phoned the nice policeman back almost immediately, well actually two days later. By then, Gloria's heels had probably cooled down. Judging by the cloying timbre of her vocal pops on the answering machine, she'd certainly learned a bit of a lesson.

"George, it's me, Gloria. I promise you I will never see that lousy plumber again. It was a one-off mistake, it meant nothing to me, nothing at all. Can you please phone some cop called Hanwick at this god-awful station and sort it all out?"

I knew that the longest they could hold her on credit card fraud without charging her was seventy-two hours. Somewhere about seventy-one-and-a-half, I called the number.

"I wonder if I could speak to Sergeant Hanwick."

"Sure, who can I say is calling?"

"George Henry. I got a message from him about a credit card thing."

"Oh yeah, sure, hang on. I'll get him right away." There was a muffling on the line, but I heard him clearly enough, shouting across the station: "Hey, Barney, it's Gloria Diner-club's sugar daddy." There was the slowly unmuffled laugh of a couple of voices, male and female, then Sergeant Hanwick came on the line.

"Hanwick speaking."

"Officer Hanwick? George Henry here. I got your message."

"Hey, thanks for calling. We have a situation here, Mr. Henry. A female Caucasian was apprehended trying to buy a Mazda, with a credit card limit of fifty bucks."

"That sounds like a real bargain of a car, Sergeant Hanwick. Surely at that price the purchaser must have been suspicious that the car was damaged in some way?"

"No. Mr. Henry, you don't understand. There was nothing wrong with the car."

"Then why get lawyers involved? Can't they just be happy with the deal and get on with their lives? We'll only make the whole situation more expensive. You know what lawyers are like?"

"Mr. Henry," he shouted across the Atlantic. "Can you just give your mind a nap for a moment and hear me out?"

"Sure," I said, helpfully.

At the end of the conversation I pretended to finally under-stand that my involvement was as guarantor of the credit card.

"Oh, I see. That Gloria Dinerman. Yes, well, I actually used to have an extramarital sexual relationship with her until quite recently." There was a short silence, then Hanwick of the police force spoke again.

"You see, she's told us that it was you who suggested to her to buy the car. Can you tell us anything about that?"

"Well, let me see now. I don't specifically recall her and I having a conversation about any particular car. But I'm pretty sure that if she'd asked me for my professional opinion, I'd have told her that a price tag of fifty dollars seemed pretty good value. Mazdas are good cars, you know, the Japanese sure know—"

"Okay, okay, thank you, Mr. Henry. You've been a great help to us with this situation."

"Have I? Well that's fantastic because that's just what I want to do, you know, just help everyone."

"So long, Mr. Henry." The tone was now a canny blend of fatigue and understanding.

"So long, Detective Hanwick," I replied, promoting him momentarily from my residence in France. I guessed they'd probably let old Gloria go without charge after that; but, to be honest, I couldn't have fucking cared less. The two-timing cow. I'd get round to reducing her limit a bit more after I got back to Boston. I knew the guy she rented her offices from, and once he knew she was under investigation for credit card fraud he'd toss her off the roof of the building himself. She wouldn't be sitting in that apartment with her binoculars at the end of September watching out for plumbers in helicopters if I had my way. Had she no compassion, the heartless bitch? Women—sometimes you can live without them.

I'd pretty much gotten a handle on the boules thing after a couple of weeks. I could feel myself beginning to unwind; and even after one phone call to Ivel, where he laid some bad news on me about some commercial deal we'd lost to a rival firm, I kinda felt like, hey, so what, that's life. This was the first holiday ever where I wasn't itching to get back to the paperwork. The heat of the sun and the whiff of dried tomatoes and barbequed pork fillets have a wonderful way of chilling you out. Even the pace of Muriel's bitching and sniping seemed to have relented a little as the holiday passed its midpoint, and we began to forget all about Boston and our lives there. When she did open her Oscar-nominated beak one Friday, it didn't provoke me the way it normally would have.

"The smell of olive oil must take you back to your childhood, George," she quipped, as we ate outside the house on the patio near the pool. Her dig at my father's lowly calling didn't bother me in the least.

"It sure does, Muriel. Thanks for helping me make the trip back down mammary lane to my mother's milk." Muriel had this thing about kids being fed draft rather than bottled milk from the get-go. She'd never really struck me as the mothering kind herself. In fact, I often wondered if she hadn't chosen Pearl as a name for her daughter to arrest any chances of being outshone by her offspring. (I have to say that I like to think I turned out pretty normal, even if I wasn't breastfed until I was twenty-four years old!)

Pearl was going to say something, but drew back at the last moment. Instead, she stuck her nose in a guidebook and invited us to share something she'd found in it.

"There's this place here called the 'Fountaine dee Vacuum' or something. I'd like to visit it. It says here it's one of the most powerful natural springs in the world. Any takers? Mom? George?"

"Pearl, maybe you could take George to see it sometime at night and have him wear lead shoes," my mother-in-law sniped.

"It's a powerful natural spring, Muriel," I said. "Maybe, if you stood on it, it could resurrect your career." I waited for a response, but none came. I looked over my shoulder at Muriel, but it was as though she hadn't heard me. Her face looked even uglier than usual as though crossed by some pain or discomfort. Pearl stood up and walked over to her.

"Mom, are you all right?"

"I'm fine, Pearl."

"It's just that you look a little—"

"I said I'm fine, Pearl," her mother rebuffed this advance of concern. She got to her feet and began to slowly walk towards the open patio doors.

"Mom?" Pearl called after her. "Are you sure you don't need some help?"

"I'm okay, Pearl. I'm not one to complain." Muriel's voice trailed into mock weakness as she entered the house.

"Not one to complain? She has a fucking degree in dissatisfaction," I said, to her fast disappearing back.

"Please, George," Pearl asked. "Leave her alone for a moment, will you?"

"Sure, honey," I replied. "I was only kidding."

"I'm worried about her, George. She's been off her food for the last couple of days."

"It's probably gas or something," I said, in a low voice that no one heard. Iska appeared in the gravel driveway, whistling merrily and with a contented look on her face. I watched Pearl to see if she had guessed the source of Iska's happiness, but I figured not.

Billy was due back in the middle of our fourth week and on that Tuesday, forty-eight hours before his return, I found myself hungry after a beer outside the hotel with Cézanne and de Gaulle. The scent of fresh bread and pastry wafted down the street at me as I made my way back up from the square towards the house. As I neared the bakery the door opened, and a woman carrying two enormous cakes stumbled out into the sunlight. The bell on the door of the shop jangled behind her and a wave of aromas escaped into the street, cutting me off in my march home. Unable to resist the temptation of an apple and strawberry pastry in the window, I caught the door before it closed. I stepped into the shop.

The main counter was glass fronted and contained every imaginable variety of pastry and cake. The artistry and attention to detail were a credit to the mastery of culinary skill which had given them life. The shop itself seemed to close in around me, and there was every shape and size of éclair and bun and birthday cake I'd ever fucking seen, and then some. It was like that film about the kids who find the golden tickets. Apart from myself, the shop was empty of customers and even the counter was unattended. I had just scooped a fingerful of orange icing into my mouth when the door behind the counter opened, and a lady wearing an apron and a paper hat—and of course all the rest of her clothes—emerged from what looked like a sitting room. I recognized her from the previous week, as the owner of the bicycle I'd seen near the war memorial. She beamed the cutest smile you ever saw and then spoke.

"Ah, Monsieur, you are the man from Montmirail, no?" (It reminded me of the man from U.N.C.L.E., but I didn't spoil the moment.)

"Yes," I replied, staring at her breasts heaving up and down behind her apron.

"I must to asking you something," she said, taking up a newspaper which lay folded to fly-swat dimensions on the work surface behind her. She walked slowly around the edge of the counter and out into the body of the shop. She opened the paper somewhat and a small headline caught my eye: LES COUSINS D'ELVIS EN VACANCES A GIGONDAS.

I remembered Herb Vissing (he'd found the place for us) telling me that he'd had to play the Elvis card to get the booking ahead of some Greek yogurt magnate.

"Are you the couzan of Elvis?" (She pronounced it 'Elveese.') I gulped as she advanced towards me (preceded by those fabulous tits).

"Yes, indeed. I sure am." I thought of old Louie, in his grave or wherever, trying to explain to the King what the actual connection between them was.

"I love Elvis," she intoned slowly.

"Oh, do you?" was the best reply I could think of.

"Yessss," she said, slowly and deliberately. "I have the most amazing collection of albums, CDs, posters of heem." She smiled.

"I bet you do."

"Would you like to see my collection?" she asked, through red lipstick, in a voice you just couldn't refuse.

I nodded, 'You bet,' aware of the biggest hard-on ever trying to trespass its way out of my pants. She reached a hand out towards me, but as I extended my own to meet it, she bypassed me completely and stretched round me to flip the sign of the shop door from OUVERT to FERMÉ.

"This way," she said in a whisper, turning to leave the shop and enter the rooms behind.

"I'm sorry," I said. "This is all wrong, I've got to go. I'm happily married. I'm not really his cousin at all." I turned and left. In my fucking toenails I did! I followed her like a ham to the slaughter. We made our way in single file through her sitting room.

At the foot of the narrow stairway, near the kitchen, was a life-size plastic statue of Elvis-Himselvis with a guitar round his neck and his hips frozen for all time in mid-thrust. My guide put one arm around the King's neck and kissed him on the permanently puckered lips. Then, with a sway of her own hips and the faint aroma of tarte-au-pomme, she began to climb the stairs. I followed, entranced by the movement up beyond and bursting to capacity with the movement below. A step creaked under my foot as we reached the top. It morphed into the beginning of a creak from the door which the bakery lady pushed into the room directly ahead. She walked in before me and as I pursued her shadowy form into near complete darkness, I wondered what the fuck I was letting myself in for.

A rustle of material, then the rasp of drawing curtains and, in a trice, the whole goddamn room was lit up. I rubbed my eyes to make sure I wasn't daydreaming but, let me tell you, I sure as hell wasn't.

"Jesus Christ!" I exclaimed.

"To me, yes, Elvis is more important than Jesus Christ," she imparted, with obvious sincerity and delight.

Talk about shrines! This room was the most shriney of shrines on the main street of Shrinesville. Elvis was abso-fucking-lutely everywhere. There were posters on every wall of the man in every imaginable jumpsuit: The Gypsy; The Blue Phoenix; The Aloha Eagle, even The Aztec 'sundial' outfit which he wore in that concert we'd seen in Indianapolis. A blown-up framed photograph of him in the barber's chair having his hair cut on entering the army adorned the back of the door. On the wardrobe, a luminous 3D picture, about two feet tall, showed him laughing on a movie set in Hawaii. I turned around and saw that the dressing table had been turned into a model of Graceland. A figure of Elvis on a motorbike sat between the plaster of Paris pillars of that great Memphis house. Something above caught my attention, and as I looked up I saw that the entire ceiling was crowded with album covers. There was barely an inch to spare. The light bulb protruded through the "50,000,000 Elvis Fans Can't Be Wrong" record sleeve with him in the gold lamé suit. So centered was the wire from the fitting, that it looked like an enormous dick hanging out of the trousers of the suit with a bulb at the end. (C'mon baby light my wire).

On the wall around the window hung a series of t-shirts from various concert tours. One announced a sold-out appearance in Rapid City, Dakota. From cradle to near-death the great man was depicted in photos, badges, t-shirts, posters, record sleeves, and every kind of memorabilia. The room was entirely devoid of furniture, except for a closet, and a stereo system sitting in one corner on a hi-fi rack under a stack of CDs as high as a fridge. Now, I'm a guy who's pretty tough to impress, but I was blown away by this room and all the paraphernalia of utter devotion to someone who was an icon at home in the States and a pretty distant relative of the mother-in-law I hated.

"You like?" she said, from behind me. I turned around to face her.

"Well, it's certainly Elvis Presley, isn't it?" I said, meaning nothing really.

"I-love-Elvis," she said slowly.

"So I see," I stuttered.

"And you, you are his couzan, you love him too?"

"Of course, sure, I mean Elvis is probably about the most famous of all my cousins."

"And you, your name is?" She advanced towards me on tiptoes.

"Um, George."

"George Presslee?"

"Well, not exactly—"

"Your name is not Presleeee?" She retreated slightly.

"Well, yes, my mother's name was Presley but my father was, uh, in the oil business, so he used his own name for legal reasons." I was now telling lies at a rate that matched my heart. She, however, seemed entirely satisfied with my explanation.

"Will you excuse me for a moment?" she asked, backing towards the door.

"Of course, sure, I'll just, well, look at old cousin Elvis."

I turned and pressed a button on a statuette of Elvis with a hound dog at his feet.

"You ain't, you ain't, you ain't," it repeated, stuck in a groove from 1956. I imagined for a second that the thing might give me away and complete its sentence by saying, "you ain't no cousin of mine," so I wrapped it in a t-shirt of Elvis on a Harley.

"Meester Presslee?" Her voice disturbed my attempt to smother the King of Rock 'n' Roll. I swung around, guiltily. The baker lady was absolutely buck naked in the doorway. She had boobs that looked like a pair of Cosmonaut apples. Her waist was so slim it must have been under pressure supporting her torso. I felt my eyes drawn down the length of her body to her tiny white feet.

"You like me?' she whispered. I could barely breathe. I tried to force the words up from my knees and through my throat up over the tonsils to the front of my mouth.

"I . . . I . . . yesss," I whispered back, more from a lack of oxygen than an attempt to reciprocate her sexy tones.

She stepped up to me and placed her left hand on my crotch and got all the answers she needed. She flicked on the light, which glowed suede-shoe blue, and re-closed the curtains. I stood transfixed, watching a thousand Elvises watching me back. I knew I shouldn't be there and yet I had no intention of leaving.

She swung the door shut. Then she kissed me on the mouth. Her tongue hinted at the insufferable pleasure to follow. As I caught my breath she broke away from the contact, and this bare sexy desirable cute petite baker flicked a switch beside the closet. The doors eased open slowly, revealing a double bed which fell silently from the wall into the center of the room. A massive pink satin bedcover bore the painted face of her hero from the *Jailhouse Rock* publicity poster. Her hand took mine and led me to the silk county prison where the warden was throwing a party. She undressed me, with a skill I'd normally imagined only Broadway show extras to possess. Next thing I knew, I was on my back with the baker preparing to put me into her oven. Somewhere in the distance, away from the erection and its reward, the stereo system kicked in and the King invited someone to let him be their teddy bear. I closed my eyes and heard the distant sound of applause from the faithful patrons of the Las Vegas Hilton as the performance began.

Dear GBH,

Here's one you might like.
MÈRE DE MÉNAGE:

A favorite exhibition variety,
by reason of its size and
remarkably Fine Color

J.A. ×××

Wolf River Apple:
dual purpose
"one apple makes a pie"
Very large, dark red flushed
Soft juicy flesh.

Isky

CHAPTER SEVEN

"The medieval method of pulping rags into paper has been recreated here, and flowers are mixed into the process to allow the paper to be colorful."

Our tour guide was an earnest English-speaking Frenchman who seemed genuinely pleased to see us. I hate those fucking types. They talk down to tourists and probably tell lies all the time. Who the hell is gonna crawl through the fucking mangle rollers to see if they use real flowers? Not G.B.H., I'm telling you. I just about managed to stay awake through the rest of the tour, with the patronizing tones of our guide resonating against the craggy rock surface of the fountain viewing-platform at the end.

"Have you any questions?" he said, as he smiled a sort of half-Camembert grin while we prepared to escape at the end of the journey. One thick moo-cow stuck her hand in the air.

"Yes?" old cheese mouth responded.

"What temperature is the water inside the cliff before it reaches the fountain?"

Can you believe it? Some people are just so dumb. This broad probably had a goddamn thermostat up her own ass and was just checking on the competition. I tuned out.

To be honest, I was exhausted; earlier that morning I'd had another workout in the Jungle Room with the baker. Her name was Carmen (like the song). An aunt had left her the bakery in her will, and so Carmen moved to Gigondas from somewhere on the coast where she'd been working in hotels as a pastry chef. She told me she'd nearly been married once, but had broken off the engagement.

"Guillaume was unwilling to share me with The Keeeng!"

I tell you, I had no such qualms. In fact, I coulda done with all the help available. She'd been a fan of the Memphis Melody Maker since she'd learned to tune her ears to anything outside herself. From what I could gather, she had a strict upbringing as a child under the guidance of a father who was a control freak. So Elvis took the place in her life of what should have been.

I found out all that during a break—while we caught our breath—before going at it hammer and tongues again, I guess you'd say. That woman knew positions that would have impressed the crowd who wrote the 'Korma Sutra.' It was a no-holds-barred rollercoaster ride of bump and grind which took me back to my late teens and early twenties (though the journey seemed to take a lot longer than it used to). She sat every which way on me and made me feel like I was the best thing that had ever happened to her. She was incredible, inexhaustible, and exuded the kind of boundless enthusiasm people usually reserve for family feuds and lottery wins. Each time I left that room above the bakery, I was in awe of my own equipment. It had moved from the 'unremarkable' category into something like the 'surprisingly able' box.

All through our bouts of lovemaking, Carmen made sure the stereo blasted out the King's hits. If I had to choose the high points of the rollercoaster ride, I'd say that two moments absolutely stand out. One was definitely taking her from behind to the strains of "Hound Dog." The other was probably watching her bob up and down on top of me during the fadeout ending of "Suspicious Minds."

At other times, when I was slipping in and out of invigorating sexually energized trances, I could hear in my head the soft incantations of some of the lesser known film soundtrack songs like "Queenie Wahine" or the gutsy blues riffs of "Power of My Love." Hey, it was just like I'd sinned and still gone to heaven. And it wasn't just the main course she excelled at, no sireee, the starters and desserts were great too. Carmen could suck the air out of a bouncy castle and still come back for the tires on your four-wheel-drive. Talk about the Fontaine de Vacuum!

It got so we had this routine each day. I'd finish the game of boules with the guys and then, round eleven thirty or so, we'd have drinks on the hotel terrace. I switched from beer to espressos just to build myself up for the activities ahead and, you know, my boules-playing improved enormously over that time, too. Carmen shut the shop from midday to one thirty, anyway, and so those windows of opportunity became the parameters of our liaison. About five or six days into our 'connection,' Carmen introduced a new aspect to the proceedings. This was presumably to keep her own interest levels up because, to tell the truth, I had no difficulty keeping anything up including my interest level. Anything but.

"Eat this," she said, climbing astride me with a pair of éclairs in her hands. She gave me one to eat while she nibbled on her own, and when mine was gone (about six seconds later) she leaned over teasingly and lowered her face to mine, so that I could eat hers as well. Suffice to say that the symbolism of the cream exploding all over our faces wasn't lost on yours truly. One morning, she even covered certain parts of herself with orange cream icing, the stuff I'd been sampling in the shop on that first day. Oh my God! is all I can say about that.

Billy got back when we had been exactly four weeks in the house. He looked great and, for the first time ever, seemed totally at ease with himself.

"Hi, Dad." He smiled as he handed me a bottle of whiskey from the duty-free shop and an envelope displaying a crest with a stag on it. "It's from Deerhunter Tours—open it, Dad," he invited.

I couldn't stand the suspense so I ripped it open.

"Dear Mr Henry,

Your luxury trip of a lifetime itinerary is enclosed."

I rummaged through the papers stapled to it and read through the catalogue of flights, transfers, and ten-star accommodations. Jesus H. Christ. Memphis, the Bahamas, and dinner in the Waldorf in New York on the last night, before a limo ride to see the Korgis' reunion in Carnegie Hall.

"Billy," I cried. "I can't believe, I just can't." I felt tears in my eyes and I let them fall. Most of them landed on Billy's shirt as I hugged him.

"Dad, forget it. It's a tiny, tiny thank you for sorting my head out and letting me sign the record deal."

"We're so proud of you, Billy," Pearl said, as she came into the room carrying a couple of plates of food that wouldn't fit onto Olivia's tray. Iska breezed into the room wearing a red Spanish-type dress Billy had bought for her, and she sashayed round the room doing twirls. It was the first time, I guess, I thought of Iska as a young lady about to take the elevator to adulthood. It was a moment for the whole family, and I just stood there looking at everyone, content in my position as head of an equally contented household.

"Billy, I hope you've stopped taking drugs." Muriel's voice invaded our momentary happy heaven. She strode into the room like a cat with a mouse stuck in its teeth and an anvil tied to its tail. The air was full of tension again, so I tried to pour oil on troubled waters.

"Muriel, do you ever shut up? Why don't you just leave Billy alone? Nothing's ever so good for you it can't be dis-improved with a little venom and bile." I waited for Pearl to come to her mom's defense, but she didn't. In fact, quite the opposite. She rallied to Billy's aid as well.

"Mom, can-you-please-butt-out? We have had a tough time in this family recently, and everybody, except you, is making an effort to help everybody else out. Why do you always have to be so negative? Why, Mom?"

I'd never heard Pearl talk to Muriel like that, and everyone—including Olivia, who didn't speak much English—seemed to grasp the feeling of the moment and get right behind Pearl and support her. Muriel looked dagger-eyed around the room in a display of last ditch defense that had long since lost any of its steam. As the rest of the family stood in silence, Muriel's face began to show signs of realizing that she was in a minority of one and she finally backed off.

"What I meant, Pearl, about Billy, is that I'm glad he's moved on from that place and those things." She sniffed a little self-pityingly and rewrote her insult into a plaudit. Pretty fucking thin, if you were asking me.

About three days later, Iska brought her boyfriend home for supper. He was a nice quiet French kid called Michel. He turned out to be Olivia's nephew.

"Are you really the cousins of Elvis?" he asked, as I bit into a cheese and ham sandwich on garlic bread. I nearly choked on the Gruyère and looked up. Pearl was smiling and Iska had put her hand on the boy's arm as if to dissuade him from this line of questioning. Muriel said nothing, so I braved the waters.

"Yes, yes. We are related to Elvis," I said with a smirk. "In fact, Muriel is the closest relative here of Elvis. Muriel is the very, very old lady over there. She's Iska's grandmother."

I watched Muriel's face go red from the neck up, as she fought against her obvious instinct to pull a gun from nowhere and blow my head off. Her face became crossed with train tracks of hatred, and she held both hands slightly above the table surface like they were hovering or something. We all waited for her to explode, yet she did not. There was some feral power inside her now, forcing her back from the brink of all-out war. It was impossible to say what that force was. I really felt that it was a bit late in the old bat's life for restraint to be making an appearance, but there it was. I recalled Pearl's concern, of a few days earlier, about her mom's health. But, to be honest, I really could not believe that anything as fortuitous as serious illness could be the case either.

"I wonder if you would all excuse me? I'm feeling a little tired," she said, pushing away from the table and getting to her feet.

She left the gathering without saying another word and, you know, it was right then that it struck me that the battle between myself and my dragon of a mother-in-law might suddenly be over. It had first manifested itself on God's earth twenty-five years earlier, with her sneering laugh (about my father's method of earning a living) on the very first day I met her at their home in Cambridge, Mass. I suppose it was inevitable, but I hadn't ever imagined that anything short of either Muriel's death (or even my own) would end the long-running war of attrition between us. In a way, I was kind of disappointed. I'd sort of been preparing for a showdown with her for years, and now it looked as if it was more high hopes than High Noon which would befit the cessation of hostilities. Oh, well—you win some, you tie some.

"Let's go to Orange, Dad. Just you and me," Billy suggested a day or two later, after I'd returned from my daily pilgrimage to the bakery. I was getting fitter now, and could feel the walk up and down the village much less in the back of my legs than when we'd arrived almost five weeks earlier. Orange is a pretty big market town near Gigondas.

"Sure, Billy."

I was glad of the opportunity to spend a bit of time alone with him, now that I'd realized he was finally grown up, and was soon to depart the family nest altogether in search of fame and fortune. We rented a car from the small garage on the road to Seguret, and Billy drove.

"How'd you get on with Ivel, about the investment side of things?" I asked, as the wind messed our hair while we drove down from the mountains along the hot dusty roads.

"Awesome, Dad. He's told me about the new block of condos being built near Fisherman's. Your firm is handling the leasing, right?"

"Yeah, they're a pretty good investment, from what I recall. What did Ivel say about them?"

"He says he can pull a few strings with the construction company and get me two of them for thirty or forty percent less than market value." Billy swerved to avoid a chicken on the road.

"So, what do you think?"

"I told him to buy them for me and to give the leasing to a local real estate firm. Ivel says that they'll provide me with an income, even if the second album never gets made."

I was proud of Billy and this display of common sense. I figured that it was important for our relationship that I be at arm's length from any decisions he made from here on out, but I also knew that Ivel wouldn't give him a bum steer. We got to Orange and parked, and wandered through the small market streets. We had a beer in a bar on the Rue St. Florent, and we talked about Billy's week in New York in the studio.

"It was amazing, Dad, you know. Like we'd been waiting for years for our chance and here it is. Hairy played the best fucking guitar riffs of his life and Joe sang his heart out. We're just, you know, so lucky that it's happened to us and we're not going to blow this shot at making it."

"Tell me about the single."

"The Pussy Farm?"

"Shhhsh." I put a finger to my lips. "Don't tell the whole world."

"They're gonna find out soon enough, if I have anything to do with it." Billy laughed. "Wanna see the sleeve design?"

"Sure."

Billy pulled a sheet of paper from his pocket and unfolded it. The design was certainly novel, I'll give them that. It depicted a stallion with an enormous erection. The horse was up on his hind legs and apparently about to get it on with some cat woman near the edge of the page, who was looking back anxiously over her shoulder. The probable point of contact was obscured by the name of the band, East Pole. Down at the foot of the activities, the name of the song brazened its way through with the letters of the words pockmarked by tiny cats peeping out here and there.

"Whaddya think, Dad?" Billy was obviously very proud. I was loath to disappoint his expectations.

"I can see how it might attract attention, alright."

"Great, Dad, I'm glad you like it. I'm gonna get it blown up and framed for you and one for Ivel."

"That's fantastic," I said, wondering secretly if this might be the catalyst for my sole ownership of the law firm. Ivel Schwartz was the kind of guy who got offended if you wore the wrong shoes. Fuck knows what this might do to his dicky ticker.

Later on, we made our way to the fifth-century Roman theater where they still held concerts.

"I'd love to play a gig here, Dad," Billy said.

"Maybe you will, Billy. Maybe you will."

"It's ironic really, Dad, but we had to fly halfway round the world to find a building that's older than Grandma." We both laughed. It was a gloriously hot sunny afternoon in Orange, and we walked round the place for a couple of hours until the day cooled down. As we drove back to Gigondas, the mountains came into view—those giant sets of fucking dentures. Billy slowed the car and pulled into the driveway entrance of an old factory.

"I gotta tell you something, Dad," he said solemnly.

"What? Is it the fucking drugs thing again?" I snapped.

"No, no, Dad. I just wanted to stop everything for a moment and say thanks for punching my lights out and locking me in that room to get that shit out of my system. I want you to know that I realize how fucking close I was to ruining my whole life. Thanks for stopping me." He hugged me and we both made brave efforts not to cry. As he started the engine up, I responded in kind.

"Think nothing of it, Billy. If you can't rely on your own father to punch you unconscious and throw you from a roof into a swimming pool, who the fuck can you rely on?" We laughed together and all was well with the world.

"I've got to find something else to replace all that junk in my life, Dad," Billy continued. "The band is great, but when I'm not playing music I'm not gonna be hanging round nightclubs or shooting light bulbs in the swimming pools like—"

"Like cousin Elvis?" I suggested.

"Abso-fucking-lutely not," he said as he grinned.

I have to say that in the immediate aftermath of that bonding afternoon with my boy, I felt a twinge of guilt for the first time about Carmen. It was like I was cheating on my whole family in a way.

"Oh, Elvis, Elvis, Elvissssssssssssssss."

Carmen roared like an opera singer, as she climaxed to the strains of "Easy Come Easy Go," and I just lay below and watched as the worshipping continued on top. She was amazing, this shy cake baker. I'd never had so much sex in my entire life, yet I felt I was enjoying it more than I ever had before with anyone. I was fifty-one and felt thirty years younger. You're probably wondering how I was able to live with the deception and lies and infidelity but, let me tell you, Gloria Dinerman hadn't crossed my mind in weeks. I know it may seem a bit hypocritical to be banging the baker, when I was supposed to be atoning for my previous indiscretions and simultaneously rebuilding my marriage. Sure, there was an element of deception, but I've never really been one to dwell on things. The truth was that things really were improving between me and Pearl, and I knew that the icing sessions with Carmen weren't going to last forever. There's no point in having a conscience you can't live with!

"Billy's been on the internet and found some sports place near the coast," Pearl said, near the end of our fifth week, as she and I had breakfast together in Gigondas for the first time.

"He told me he was looking for some interests outside of music to keep him sane," I said, scooping raspberry jam out of a croissant where I'd mistakenly deposited it moments earlier.

"He's grown up a lot lately, George." Pearl smiled and laid down her coffee cup near mine.

"He sure has."

"And most of it is thanks to you." She put her hand on my arm.

"No, not really. He's had to make all the choices himself, Pearl."

"But you helped him make those choices, George."

Pearl's voice was kinder now than I'd recalled it being in years. She rubbed my arm gently, and I realized that the shadow of my tryst with old Gloria Diningroom had begun to lift from between us. Now, to be fair, it may well have been that the half of that shadow which lay closest to me had been blown away by the baker opening the curtains in that temple to His Presleyness just above the bakery—only a few hundred yards away from Montmirail, with its shimmering pool and candles stuck in wine bottles.

Pearl confirmed my suspicions about the demise of the darkness between us by opening the Pearly gates, so to speak, and renewing the physical commitment of our union that same night. As we lay side by side, after the best sex we'd ever had, she commented on my performance.

"All that walking and playing boules is really paying off, George. I'd forgotten what a tiger you were. That was fantastic."

"Grrr," I growled, and rolled over towards her with my claws in peak condition and ready to pounce again.

"Splat, splat."

The consistency of the soapy liquid from the container in Carmen's bathroom suggested the work ahead of me as I cleaned the grime of the boules game from my hands. This was the Saturday of our last week in Provence. The sun was splitting the rocks outside, and I knew that my own rocks would be receiving like treatment shortly from the pastry queen of Provence. I looked at myself in the mirror and thought that even though I wasn't really the Casanova type, I was in receipt of more female attention now than I'd ever gotten in my whole time on this sun-kissed, bikini-mad earth.

Billy was in good shape too, and was even talking about visiting some adventure center in the Camargue (wherever that was) before we returned home at the end of the week. Old Gooch Silverspoon—or whatever—had been on the phone earlier that day, raving about the single. There was a good chance of the song being showcased on national TV at some music award ceremony in Madison Square Garden the day before we were due home. It might mean Billy would have to fly back a couple of days early, but it seemed to me like he had made a quantum leap in maturity in the last month, and really was intent on grasping this opportunity with both hands. Iska was happy. Her latest notes on apples seemed to confirm her new-found confidence. The note spoke of "Wolf River" apples and said that it had a dual purpose in the States: "One apple makes a pie." I was no closer to understanding the notes, but I have to say that my view of Iska as someone who needed looking after had moved on considerably. Muriel had finally shut up and Pearl was back in the marital bed, so the doomsday scenario, of divorce and lonely old age, now seemed like the distant threats of fictional warriors.

The intro to the Madison Square Garden Concert of 1972 was blaring as I got back to the bedroom. Carmen turned down the music and handed me a wrapped gift which was about the size of a large cushion.

"What is it?" I asked.

"It's for you, George, I made these for you," she said suggestively; and although I was anxious to open it, my eyes were mainly drawn to her black lace bra and panties which were emblazoned with the TCB logo of Elvis's with a lightning rod.

Taking care of business? Was she what? I set the parcel on the floor and as I unwrapped it, Carmen began to undress me with startling efficiency given my own state of activity. Her arms seemed to be all around me and under me and everywhere as I managed to unravel the package from about forty miles of scotch tape.

"Jesus H. Christ!" I exclaimed, as I unfolded the bundle to reveal a huge jumpsuit, complete with detachable cape showing an embroidered eagle on it.

"Do you like it?"

"I, I can't believe—"

"Please, try it on. I hope it is to be the fitting for you," she said anxiously, as she turned down the stereo.

I hesitated for about two seconds, then I slipped off my shoes and began to step into it.

"One moment," she said, reaching out to stop me as I lifted my foot to try it on. She slid my boxer shorts off so that I would be naked under the suit.

"Well, I suppose it might be a little hot in there," I agreed. Naked for a second, I pulled on the skin and cover of the King of Rock and Roll, and it fitted as though it had been made for me. I mean, I know it had been made for me, but you get the picture.

It was snow white with a royal blue pleat at the end of the trouser legs and on the cuffs of the sleeves. It was studded all over with semi-precious stones, all sewn on individually with care and skill that to me was as mesmerizing as it was alien. A zip ran from the waist to the collar, and the few hairs on my chest avoided mischief as Carmen zipped me up. The music reemerged now with the drum snaps of "Power of My Love" underpinning the slow rhythm of the guitar chords which pushed the song up and out into the room.

"Can I take your photograph?" Carmen asked.

"No, no, absolutely not; you know I just want to enjoy this with you, no photographs please." I imagined the mayhem a snap of me in this costume might create. Carmen began to sing along with the lyrics.

"Crush it, kick it, you can never win. I know baby you can't lick it, I'll make you give in. Every minute, every hour . . ." The stereo was back up to full blast.

Carmen began to dance around me now, rubbing up against me in a questioning manner which could only have one answer. As she wound her way up and around me, her hand strayed in the direction I'd hoped. I wondered how we'd manage anything, as the zip only went to the waist, but I soon found out. A small and un-resistant Velcro fastener opened my body to the air at just the right position. The high tones of the Sweet Inspirations and J. D. Sumner and the Stamps Quartet groaned at us from the 1970's.

The baker was on her knees now, and I remembered Billy's promise (not to blow his opportunity) as Carmen began to do just that to mine. Didn't I think of Pearl and her honest attempts to revive our marriage, at that point? Didn't I worry about the example I was setting for my own children with this display of wanton infidelity? No way, José! When a pretty woman twenty years younger than you has your dick in her mouth by mutual consent, you don't bother your brains with complex moral dilemmas. No siree, you just lie back (or in my case, lean slightly) and close your eyes and thank your fucking lucky stars. As far as the bakery-lady thing went, I guess you could say I wanted to have my cake and have it eat me too. "Suspicious Minds" began to play on the sound system.

FLASH! Fuck. What was that? I opened my eyes but couldn't see for a couple of seconds. Two or three more flashes in succession lit up the room. Elvis was only halfway through the second chorus when the wires on the stereo were ripped out of the wall and thrown across the room like a whip. The stars cleared, and I became aware of Carmen unsuccessfully trying to stifle my member from arriving prematurely.

Muriel stood in the doorway with a camera. She raised the Nikon to her face to capture my rapture forever, as I came uncontrollably in the most bizarre circumstances you wouldn't wish on your worst enemy. The music died, too. Carmen stayed on her knees and tried her best to look angry but, in fact, seemed on the edge of laughing. Muriel spoke menacingly.

"George Baxter Henry, what have you got to say for yourself now?"

I gulped.

"Would you say that, on balance, you prefer the version of 'Suspicious Minds' with or without the backup vocals?"

I wouldn't have thought it possible for her to become more enraged, but she did. Her face lit up like a warning light on the Titanic "holes-in-the-hull" meter. She was choking with rage, but not enough to actually choke. She spat out at me the very words I'd had nightmares about.

"Your marriage is over, George. And you're about to become bankrupt."

She turned and left me in my rhinestone jumpsuit with nowhere to jump. Oh, my sweet fucking eagle cape!!!

Chapter Eight

I got out of the suit as fast as I could. Even Elvis, at the change-around after the matinee show in the Las Vegas Hilton, could not have out-jumpsuited me on that sunny but embarrassing afternoon in Provence. I pulled on my clothes.

"Where are you going?" Carmen hollered after me as I careered down the stairs and fell, landing on top of the King in mid-thrust.

"To try and save my law firm," I roared back, as I exited the cake shop.

Once I was out on the street there was no sign of Muriel. I reckoned she'd go back to the house using the conventional route, so I had to try and head her off. I opened the first garden gate I came to, and sprinted down the side of a house into a small yard. I vaulted the back wall like a chicken on springs and landed, feet first, in a swimming pool. I recognized the turreted house at the other end of the garden as being directly opposite our own. Like Burt-fucking-Lancaster, in that movie about swimming pools, I doggie-paddled to the other end and got out, soaking wet. Just then, an old man on a ride-on mower came out of a shed to my right. He motioned angrily at me. I'm not sure what happened next, but it ended up with me trying to outrun the mower up to the back of the house to where a Doberman was tied by a chain to a concrete block. It was clear to me that if the old guy got to the dog before I got to the gate, then all of my problems would be over (except for only in that kind of awful way you never want). I reached the side of the house and a small green door lay between me and the outside non-dog world. It was locked. I overturned some antique-looking half-barrel that had angels carved on it. I stood on it to climb the wall. I heard the sound of angels grinding into the pavement, simultaneously with the scrape of nails and the woof of death behind me. I tell you, I could feel that mutt's breath on my fucking ankles as I scrambled over and out onto the street. I lost one of my shoes in the process, and took the other one off and threw it back over the door at the barking dog. For once in my life, a direct hit! The Doberman yowled. I danced up the avenue on the hot gravel fully expecting to see Pearl in tears at the door with her bags packed. No sign. Then I remembered that she had been talking about going shopping with Billy. She wanted to get him new clothes for the publicity shots that the record company had phoned him about the day before. They were sending a photographer to take some photos of him in France for an article in their in-house publication. I met Olivia in the hall.

"Ah, Monsieur Henry," she said, looking me up and down as I dripped all over the floor.

"The old lady?" I asked. She pointed upstairs and I could hear the sounds of clumping overhead.

"Madame Henry? Billy? Iska?"

"All to the shopping," she replied. I could have hugged her.

I dashed upstairs and changed into dry clothes and began the hunt through my suitcase. I found what I wanted: a faded red ring-back binder with the words 'Silent Scream Star' written on the cover. I combed my hair and put on a jacket and then rummaged for a tie in the drawers, and found one with the crest from the Law School of San José, my alma mater. A last look in the mirror, and I was as ready as I was ever going to be. I took a couple of deep breaths and started down the stairs. Standing on the fifth or sixth step from the bottom, I could see the suitcases packed and piled up in the hall. The door of the living room was slightly ajar, and I pushed it open further and stepped into the dragon's lair. She was at the other end of the room in an armchair with her arms folded. On her head she sported the ridiculous hat I'd last seen her wear at Billy's christening.

"Muriel?" Silence. Then I spoke again. "Muriel, I wonder if I could have a word with you, please?"

She ignored me and looked straight ahead out through the front window, waiting for her daughter.

I walked into the middle of the room and blocked her view. I tried again, "Muriel?" This time she beat me to the punch.

"George, you and I have nothing to discuss. I am waiting for my daughter and my grandchildren to return, and then we are leaving for the airport. There's a flight at seven."

"Muriel, Muriel, listen to me. We have to talk. There are a couple of things I need to ask you."

"You need to ask me something, George? How dare you? You're nothing but a two-timing gutless weasel of a failed lawyer from olive oil stock, George. There's nothing more to say."

"Oh, but I think there is, Muriel," I said firmly, moving backwards towards the door. "I have a couple of questions to ask you. It shouldn't take long." I produced the bound file from under my arm.

"You little whippersnapper, don't you dare raise your voice to me." She stood up and walked a couple of steps in my direction. I opened the file and flicked to the first page.

"Let's begin with Carole Lombard, shall we?" I said softly. Muriel stopped and looked at me and at the papers I held in my hands.

"Begin wherever and with whomsoever you wish, George. But I'm not going to answer any of your silly questions."

"That's a pity, Muriel. Because everybody is entitled to a fair trial and—"

"A trial? What on earth do you mean by that, George? You haven't seen the inside of a courtroom for—"

"I know, I know, twenty years or more. But you know what, Muriel? I'm still pretty good at putting a case together. Of course, if you'd prefer, I can simply hand over the information to Pearl and let her make up her own mind."

"About what?" I clearly had her interest, at least momentarily.

"About you, Muriel, of course." I stood aside to let her leave the room, but she wasn't leaving now.

"What about Carole Lombard?" she said, in an I-couldn't-care-less voice which said I-couldn't-care-more.

"Well," I said, moving back into the center of the room. "Why don't you take a seat and we can clear up these historical details before Pearl comes back."

"You mean, before I show her the photographs of her husband having—"

"Oral sex?" I suggested. She didn't even dignify me with a "thank you."

"I'm going to tell Pearl all about you and your little pastry-puffer, George. There's absolutely nothing you can say or do to change that. Unless, of course, you're prepared to murder me, which I wouldn't think even you are capable of. Or, have you some hidden reserves of strength and purpose we've missed all these years?"

"You hold onto your Polaroids, Muriel, and do whatever you want with them. All I'm interested in is your own glittering career, and there are just a few things which need to be clarified for your biography."

"A biography?" She was beside her original chair now and sat down again.

"Not that anyone's writing an official one, Muriel. Nothing as incredible as that. No, this is just, let's say, a family history. I've got some notes I've kept about things you've told us over the years. I just want to straighten them out in my own mind before I can do anything formal like write a book about your life and your career, et cetera, et cetera." I could see the interest welling up now behind her eyes, and blending with her irrepressible ego at the thought of posterity being bothered by a biography of Muriel Hale.

"I'm happy to indulge you for a few minutes, George. This will probably be our last ever conversation together, although we'll almost certainly meet at the divorce hearing. Carole Lombard?"

"Yes, Carole Lombard. You've told us that you spent a vacation with her in Miami just before you started shooting the movie, Mr. . . ."

". . . and Mrs. Smith," she said, patronizingly.

"Correct. Now, from my research, that movie was shot at the RKO Studio in Burbank from April eleventh until May thirty-first, nineteen forty-one."

"So what?"

"Bear with me. When did you return from Miami? Was it the day before shooting began? A week earlier? Two weeks? Now, if you can't remember just say so."

"I remember all right, George. Lucile Watson hosted a party on the weekend before filming began, and we arrived that evening from Miami in Carole's car."

"Who drove to the party?"

"Carole did. I don't recall the make or model or number of the car, George, but I hope you're satisfied by the rest of the details."

"As a matter of fact, no, I'm not. You see, the information I have is that Carole Lombard had broken her leg in an auto accident four weeks before shooting began. In fact, Harry Edington, the producer, insisted that she appear for the first three days on the set with her leg in a cast so that scenes other than full length could be shot. All of her action scenes were put off until the last ten days of the production."

"I don't believe you. What you're saying is—"

"That you couldn't have been on vacation with her in Miami, and she certainly couldn't have driven to the party with her leg in a cast."

"Don't be ridiculous, George. I was there, you weren't even born. I know the facts." She snapped in an offhand way that I did not find at all convincing.

"I thought you might react like this, Muriel. Are you saying she wasn't in a cast? Or didn't have the accident? Or you were on holiday with her and she did drive the car? You still stand by all of those "facts" as you call them?'

"Absolutely, it's all true." She folded her arms.

"Then perhaps you'd like to have a look at this, Muriel." I handed her a sheet of paper.

"What is it?" she asked, before accepting possession of Exhibit A.

"It's a copy of the hospital admission record. You'll see that it contains the date of the plaster-of-Paris cast being put on. That appears to be March third 1941, and it was removed on the nineteenth of May 1941."

"You could have typed this yourself on an old typewriter, George. It's absolutely worthless." She tossed the paper aside. I picked it up and replaced it in the file.

"I could have typed it, but I didn't, Muriel," I said, taking out the next page from the folder and handing it to her.

"What's this?" she asked dismissively.

"A letter from the current head of administration at the hospital, certifying the record as an authentic copy of the original." I let her read it, then I snatched it back. "But, of course, that could be another forgery, couldn't it, Muriel? Well, the lady has very kindly provided me with her phone number in case she can be of further help. I'm sure Pearl could phone her to check."

"And I could simply say to Pearl that I remember it the way you've told me now, and that your 'records' simply confirm my own recollection." She grinned in an evil manner.

"You could. But even that wouldn't explain why in the first place you said you were on vacation with her when it's quite clear you weren't."

"You don't know that."

"I don't, but I can find out. Can you provide me with the name of the hotel you stayed in, the airline you used to fly to Miami, times and dates of departure and arrival, Carole Lombard's home address?" Muriel looked angry but said nothing.

"Okay." I smiled. "Enough about Carole Lombard. Let's move on to some other people you claim to have known." I began to flick through some pages and stopped at a black and white photograph of Marlene Dietrich.

"That's mine," she snarled. "Where did you get it?"

"Don't you remember? You gave it to Pearl on the day Marlene Dietrich died in 1992. I'd been out drinking with Herb Vissing. It was our wedding anniversary and I forgot all about it."

"May sixth," she said bitterly, as though she'd been married to me herself.

"Yep," I said. "I forgot the anniversary, so you gave her this, a lifelong treasure from your own career. It's signed, 'To Muriel, hugs and kismet. M.D. 1943.'"

"So?"

"Where did she sign it? Was it on a film set, or did someone get it for you secondhand?"

"How dare you? I met with Marlene at MGM during one of the breaks. I was at the studio meeting some people from publicity."

"So you met her?"

"Met her? I knew her. We were great friends. We both had our hair permed by Sidney Guilaroff. That's how close we were."

"It's a forgery," I said.

"You bastard, how can you denigrate the name of Marlene Dietrich? She was a goddess, an angel, you know nothing of her, absolutely nothing."

I ignored her ranting and produced a letter from a hand-writing expert in the CIA who had been in law school with me.

"Here. Read it for yourself, Muriel. '99.7% certainty that it is not her handwriting.' If you read on, you'll see that he has done about a dozen comparisons from signatures on contracts at MGM and remarks that nowhere else does she ever sign herself, 'M.D.' It's a classic way to forge autographs; have a personal message and just use the famous person's initials. Of course you never meant to sell the thing, your purpose was much more personal. That's why you reckoned it would never be tested. Giving it to Pearl on our anniversary was the perfect way to use it to persuade her that—"

"That what, George? What was I trying to persuade her of?"

"That you are the person you pretend to be: an actress, a star who rubbed shoulders with stars and who achieved great-ness herself."

"I was a great actress, George. I was nominated for an Academy Award."

"I know, I know. We'll get to that later, Muriel. But I note you don't deny that the signature is a forgery. Let's move on, shall we?"

"If you like, George. You can continue this farce of a cross-examination, but I'm a ninety-one-year-old lady and I don't have to take this kind of amateur historical revisionism from anyone. I bet Pearl will be shocked when she finds out." She got up from the chair and began to stride toward the door.

"I'm afraid she will, Muriel. I'm afraid she will. She's going to be very shocked indeed when she reads what I've found out by doing a little digging."

I heard the footsteps stop (if you know what I mean), and then I turned around slowly to see Muriel's face crossed with a pallor that was right out of *Funeral Weekly*. She put one hand behind her to feel for the door and pushed it closed. It clicked shut, and then a glance passed between us that meant we both understood the game now. That small noise of a door shutting in France at the tail end of August was like a starter's gun for the confrontation that we had both always known to be inevitable. The rules were clear. I had until Pearl returned to continue my questioning, and Muriel would ultimately be judge and jury as to the value of the information presented or the admissions elicited. Twenty years of my lack of experience in the courtroom would now face its toughest test.

I'd been collecting information about Muriel since even before our wedding day. Up until recently though, the final pieces of my investigation had not really been complete. Allied to that, I must confess that I'd never really had either the opportunity or the guts to produce my folder and cut loose. Any such doubts were now cast aside as I had no other choice; it was do or divorce. The witness returned to the stand and the lawyer resumed the cross-examination.

"Charles Chaplin." I announced.

"What about him?"

"You claim to have been asked by him to play the female lead instead of Virginia Cherrill in *City Lights* in 1931?"

"That's true."

"Is it? You said that you were under contract at RKO and they wouldn't release you for the part."

"Correct."

"But RKO didn't renew your contract after *Brooklyn Bridge* a year earlier, did they?"

"I was under contract, and Wilfred Kaufmann refused to release me to make pictures for anyone else."

"I'm not sure that's quite true, is it? My understanding is that you and Kaufmann parted company shortly after the Oscars in 1930, the previous year."

"I don't know what you mean, George." She had a haughty attitude, but it was cracking. I reached for the evidence and showed her a whole quarter-page article in the *LA Times* of July 1930 which was headlined: RKO'ED: HALE FALLS FROM GRACE.

The tears started to well up in her eyes now, but she somehow managed to kinda suck them back in.

"Can you explain this, Muriel?" I waved the headline at her and began to read. "'Hollywood was shaken today after RKO announced the termination of the six-picture contract it signed in December of last year with Oscar-nominated Muriel Hale. In a press statement—'"

"Alright, alright. So, I was let go. We had a disagreement, a row about—"

"Don't tell me, artistic differences, Muriel?"

"Yes. I wouldn't expect you to understand anything about Art, George."

"But I do understand about times and dates and lies, Muriel. I'm afraid you've spun us quite a lot of tall stories over the years about your career. Let me continue. Clark Gable. You say you starred with him in *The White Sister* in 1933. I'm afraid that despite my very best efforts to locate you in that movie, there's no sign of you. I rented the video recently and you don't even get a credit."

"That's outrageous. I never told you that I was in that movie. I said I auditioned for that movie."

"Funny you should change your story now, but it's actually recorded on our wedding day when Dick Grobbe taped the speeches. You warbled on for ten minutes and listed that as one of your film credits. I have a transcript of the tape here if you'd like to see it." She didn't want to.

"Are you quite finished?" She looked at her nails in a show of apparent boredom.

"No, I'm not, Muriel. In fact, I'm only getting to the good parts now. What about your Oscar nomination?"

"My nomination? What the hell are you trying to insinuate about my nomination, George? You're a cruel, spiteful man."

"Steady on with plaudits, Muriel, my girl. You're not too shy in the hate and cruelty department yourself, if I'm not mistaken."

"What do you mean?"

"Well, I did a little searching through some files and libraries in Los Angeles over the years, but I never could find anything to link you to the process of Oscar nominations until just a few months ago. I did some digging and I discovered a very interesting little item." I watched her now and she began to blush. Ever so slightly at first, but the color intensified as I whispered the magic name, "Christopher Power."

"What? I don't know any directors with that name." She was panicky.

"Who said he was a director, Muriel? Not me."

"No, no, I didn't mean that I knew him, it's just that the name, the name is . . ." She was hyperventilating now.

"Yes, the name 'Christopher Power' is a business alias of Steven Hardone, who directed your fabulous picture. 'Christopher Power Limited' was the company used to front the bribing and blackmail of the Academy, or at least enough of them to swing the nomination. I think I'm right in saying that, Muriel? I only made the connection when I read the newspaper reports from the time, about the whiff of scandal in relation to the nomination process. The trail stopped cold at a recently formed company with a fictitious address. But I managed to find out, through a legal research firm in California, that there was an investigation by the DA's office in the same period into corporate fraud and tax evasion. It revealed some very interesting information and names and addresses."

"You can't prove anything, this is all speculation." She was defiant now—like the wasp on its back which still thinks it has enough energy to fire the sting.

"The address used for the corporate tax return was your home address, Muriel. Incidentally, this was the same address given by Hardone when he was arrested the following year for drunk driving. You were being boned by him, weren't you, Muriel?"

"My private life is absolutely none of your concern. Who do you think you are, snooping into other people's pasts and making horrible and false allegations?"

"But they're not false, are they, Muriel? You were having an affair with this guy and he put you into his picture. Maybe you even got the screen test without having to give him a good time, but it's absolutely clear that RKO wanted nothing to do with either of you when they found out. You were a small-time actress who got a break and blew it—or rather, found a director and blew him. You moved on to Louie then, and he was your meal ticket right up until he died."

"I loved Louie," she sobbed.

"Maybe you did love Louie, Muriel. But it seems he wasn't enough for you either."

"What do you mean?" The crying stopped like a faucet being turned off. She looked startled.

"Louie wasn't Pearl's father, was he?" I asked calmly.

Outside, the sound of the taxi bringing Pearl, Iska and Billy back crunched up the gravel driveway. Pearl would be in the house in moments. I pulled out another page from the book of evidence.

"What do you—?" she began, but I silenced her with my hand in the air and passed the information to her.

"Blood type," I said. "I had a look at Louie's autopsy report and it says AB negative. He couldn't possibly be Pearl's father."

"But when did you . . . ?"

"I started looking right after you advanced the money to Pearl so I could buy into the partnership. I found out that the Register of Bequests had you down for a load of dollars from the estate of this guy Hardone a couple of years earlier. I reckoned no one would be so stupid as to leave money to a person fifty years later who wasn't family, unless he'd rattled his saber at you sometime. The rest is . . ."

"The rest is guesswork, George," she said, simply.

"You're right there, Muriel. But that's what intuition is—pure guesswork. My guess is, you didn't have the guts to leave Louie, because Hardone was never going to leave his wife."

"Pearl won't even listen to this, this bullshit. Once she knows about you and that cup-cake whore. She won't even . . ."

"Speaking of whores," I said, as I played the final card of the hand it had taken two decades plus to build. It was a hazy enough photograph of a police raid on the Emerald "Entertainment" Club in February 1934, but the effect was instantaneous. The fox-like eyes of this insufferable nonagenarian narrowed in absolute fear. I could hear the children and Pearl in the kitchen with Olivia now. They'd be with us in seconds.

"What happens now, George?" The old dragon asked for terms.

"Here's the deal, Muriel. You keep your mouth shut from now until the coffin-makers arrive. Don't ever utter a single word about my marriage, my infidelities, my qualifications, my lack of trial experience. In fact, don't ever fucking criticize me again. In return, your grandchildren will never get to find out that you humped your way to a bogus Oscar nomination, made fewer personal appearances than Salman Rushdie, and Pearl will always believe that Louie was her father. So it means she's not directly related to Elvis but, hey, you can't have everything. Oh, and speaking of Elvis, nobody need ever see my jumpsuited performance or your own Viva Los Angeles appearance at the Emerald Club. Perhaps it's time for you to go silent again, Muriel. The talkies never really suited you."

"Mom? Where are you?" Pearl's voice sounded through the door like the end of a dream as I waited for Muriel to decide. The door swung open and Pearl was in the doorway, standing between forever and me.

"Why are these suitcases packed? Mom, what's going on?" Pearl's face was covered in worry. I coulda bitten my fucking wrist off with the tension. Muriel rose slowly from the witness box to deliver the decision. ("Have you reached a verdict on which you are all agreed?")

"I've decided to take Iska to Avignon for a few days, Pearl. Billy's flying home early, so I really think that you and George should have some time together, alone. After all, that's what you came here for in the first place."

Pearl turned around to call up the stairs for Iska. As Muriel went out of the room past me, she handed me an envelope with the Polaroids. I burned them that evening and, no, I didn't fucking keep one for posterior. I was free again. Good old Liberty, Equality, Paternity!

CHAPTER NINE

"You see this place, Dad? It's amazing."

I looked over Billy's shoulder at the gleamy screen of his laptop filled with flashing photographs of expensive cars and helicopters.

"What is it, Billy?"

"It's this awesome place called Au Fond du Monde. It means like the edge of the universe, or something." Billy clicked an icon with his mouse, and the screen changed to reveal the stilted image of someone falling from a plane without a parachute. "It's just amazing, Dad. This place has got sports, adventures and the most incredible edge-of-this-fucking-world activities. And it's right here in France."

"Are you thinking of paying a visit to it?"

"Am I what? Absolutely, Dad. I'm gonna scoot down there day after tomorrow and see what's cooking. I could really dig some of those activities."

"Be careful, Billy," I warned. "Some of those things look pretty dangerous."

"Lighten up, Dad. What could be more dangerous than trying to snort two tons of cocaine in between cramming for Bolivian history exams?"

"Oh," I said. "I got a message from the college at the office yesterday. Judy told me that they wanted to know if you're going back in the Fall for the repeat exams. I told her to call them and say you were quitting to become a rock star, so don't let me down now."

"I won't, Dad. I talked to Hairy and Joe last night by e-mail and they said that the publicity's really heating up in New York. The single's out this week. You know, I still can't quite believe it's all happening—really happening."

"Believe it, Billy, and savor every goddamn moment, because it won't last forever. The best things rarely do."

"You've lasted a long time, Dad. What's your secret? You must be nearly what, seventy?" he joked.

"Get outta here, I'm closer to forty than I am to seventy."

"I guess they keep moving it, huh?" Billy laughed loud and long, and I was as proud as hell of him. What parent wouldn't be?

Pearl was even happier than I was, about her mom taking a hike to Avignon for a few days.

"Oh, George, I'm so glad to have you all to myself for a change," she said, as she arrested my dressing habits one morning and led me back to the bed for some unexpected connubial exertions.

"I don't think you've really had to share me with your mom," I said, as I laughed.

"No, not Mom. The kids. Everything. Well, it's all beginning to work out so well, George. Don't you think so, too?"

To be fair, when you're getting more sex than you ever reckoned you could handle, and it's hot outside as well, and divorce is on the most recent train outta town, I gotta admit it's pretty close to working-out-so-well.

"I do, Pearl, I do," I replied, feeling slightly out of breath. The sex had improved in quality as well as frequency. Those smart-assed young lawyers from downtown Boston with their Rolex watches and racquetball coaches woulda been hard pressed to process any more loveabilia than I did that summer. I had begun to ease out of the situation with Carmen, but with the action at home on the increase, the overall volume was down very little, if at all.

"You don't visit every day now," Carmen complained later that week, as I snaffled some cream from the cakes in the shop. We began to trek upstairs, past the wounded figure of Elvis I had injured in my haste to race Muriel back to the house only days earlier.

"Well, Carmen, I have to be more careful now with—"

"Your wife?" she suggested, in a hurt voice like I was actually cheating on her or something by sleeping with Pearl. Can you believe these broads?

"Yes, I've got to be careful about things now. We're going back to Boston on Sunday." Carmen looked a little surprised.

"Boston? I thought that you were to be the staying to be ze buying of the house?"

Oh Christ, I thought. Just what I need, another fucking sexual dependent.

"Yes, yes, of course, Carmen. But there are lots of things to sort out back in America. I have to think about my business, but, of course, there will be other holidays here in Gigondas."

"Holidays? You said that you were going to live here for always, George Preslee."

She looked mad now, and I understood why. I recalled that, in a particularly weak moment some weeks earlier, I had sort of imparted to Carmen a vague intention to move to Gigondas at some near point in time and to continue our liaison. I might even have spoken of divorcing Pearl. Carmen also knew, through the local newspaper, of our option to purchase the place. To be honest, I was stunned that she'd really believed me. I began to see now the classic signs of infidelity going horribly wrong.

It's such a fucking mess when trust and expectation intrude on afternoon sex. It's like water seeping into a ship; the meaning of 'going down' changes completely. Suddenly it's all "me," "me," "me," instead of the inherent selflessness of the liaison itself. How could I have been so blind and altruistic as to imagine that the calm, detached warmth and honesty I'd brought to the baker's table would be ultimately thrown back in my face—marinaded in commitment and demand? Oh, the caring professions, where do we get our grace? I didn't want her calling round and ruining everything, though.

"Yes, Carmen, and I will be coming back. But there is so much to organize. I mean, we have to get back to our home in Boston and sell that house and sort out my divorce first. Then I'll be able to come back, and you and I can make arrangements perhaps to be—"

"Married?" She whooped. "I will be Mrs. Preslee, Madame Preslee?"

"Maybe, yes," I lied, putting my head in my hands. "But first I must get a divorce and think of the children, and of course, the business will have to be sold. I'm very tired, Carmen. I have so much to think about, so much to organize. I cannot let Pearl find out about you. The old lady almost told her everything. You must trust me to do this in my own way."

"Yes, George, I understand, you have very much to do," she agreed. "Please let me help you relax," she said, heading in the direction of the lower deck of the jumpsuit where only flapping Velcro stood between happiness and me.

"Oh, oh," I groaned, encouraging her in her endeavors. I'd have to pack pretty soon.

I was definitely going to have to get rid of Carmen from my life A.S.A.P. But I had to be careful about how I did it. The last thing I wanted was some fucking scene down at the house, now that Muriel was out of the way and Pearl and I had reached a level of understanding which looked certain to be enough to save our marriage (oh yeah, and of course, my financial hide). I was pretty proud of myself, all right, the way things had turned out. Billy had grown up all of a sudden and Iska was well on her way to adulthood. I was surer than I'd ever been that she was anything but "a little slow." Of all of us, she seemed the only one who hadn't had to undergo all manner of stress and strain to reach out and scoop a handful of water from the fountain of contentment.

I suppose I couldn't really believe the luck I'd had in facing down Muriel with the stuff from her past. I had spent a good many hours over the years checking out this and that, and jotting down the snippets of "facts" she'd fed us for decades about how great an actress she was.

Actors. God. They gave me a royal pain in the ass even before I'd met Muriel. I knew this one prick from college in San José in the drama club, Jack Harvey. At least, I think that's what his name was. He was such a prick that if there were a shortage of pricks he'd make two. He was always walking around the campus "getting into character" as he called it, wandering about, talking aloud, and having these imaginary conversations on his own where he was always, like, taking offense or something: "How dare you?" or, "I can't believe you're standing there telling me that."

He was such a pretentious moron. You'd see him in the cafeteria with his head stuck in some notebook, like he was writing the great American novel or something. The thing about this guy was it was all show; when you actually got to see him in action, he was awful. He was worse than awful, actually, because he was so bad playing other characters he was almost like—well, if you could imagine—he was like Hamlet playing Jack Harvey instead of the other way around. You know, what I always wondered was, if these guys were such great actors, then why don't they just find a part where the person is a decent soul instead of a prick, and then "get into" that character and fucking well stay there? All great ideas are simple, yeah?

"YEAA-YESSSSSSS-YES-YES," Billy's voice echoed through that old French house on the morning of the day he was leaving for the edge-of-your-seat theme-park place. His cry brought Pearl and myself together in the hall from opposite ends of the house.

"What is it, Billy?" I asked, as he put down the phone. His face was a mix of delirium and wonder.

"The single, the single," he chanted, jumping up and down like a man with pogo sticks instead of feet.

"What about the single?" Pearl pitched in.

"We're in the Top Ten, the fucking Billboard Top Ten."

"In the charts? Hey, Billy, that's fantastic." I threw my arms around him.

"Number eight, number eight, number eight," Billy sang to the unoriginal tune of "Here We Go," etc. "The new chart will be announced on Sunday, so we might get to Number One."

My son was in the charts and everything was right with the world.

"Oh, Billy, we're so proud of you," Pearl sobbed, as the three of us hugged in the hall.

"And you know the best thing of all?" Billy came up for air.

"No," we both answered.

"The video has been banned by ninety percent of the TV channels in the U.S. and here in Europe."

"And that's good?" Pearl was uncomprehending.

"Sure, Mom. Nothing sells quicker than something the government doesn't want you to have."

"The government? What has it got to do with the single?" Pearl showed her age.

"It's a figure of speech, Mom," Billy said, grinning.

"Yeah, just a figure of speech, Mom." I echoed my son the rock star's coolness.

This was bliss; my family around me (well two of them, anyway), and the scent of success in the air. I wasn't yet sure as to how I was going to extricate myself from the bakery without getting too much flour on my hands. But I'd work that out before we left, or just after we got home. Iska and Muriel were due back on Saturday, and we were flying Sunday, so there were only a couple of days left really to tie things up. Billy had to be in New York on Friday night for the awards ceremony. They were the guest artists for the event and would perform their song live in front of an invited audience of stars, and a television viewership which was expected to top twenty million. I wondered how many people had seen the *Aloha from Hawaii via Satellite* special in 1973. On the other hand, perhaps it was a bit premature for comparisons. The cat song had only just jumped out of the door-flap at the world. Now we would all just have to wait to see how big a splash it made on landing.

I played my final game of boules on Thursday morning, just after Billy had left in a rental car to go to the place in the Camargue. Old Pinochet, de Gaulle and Cézanne were off to the coast to play in some tournament over the weekend, and I told them I would not be in Gigondas when they returned the following week.

"Goodbye, M'sieu," they each said solemnly in turn, as they shook my hand when the game had ended. They presented me with a brand new glittery set of boules.

"Au revoir, mes grandes amis," I read, from a phonetically-spelled prompt card which Carmen had helped me to write. They seemed suitably impressed. We exchanged addresses. (Well, they gave me theirs and I handed them details of a place I'd lived in Los Angeles some thirty years earlier.) I was very anxious to make sure Carmen would have no leads to follow if she began to sniff the trail after it dawned on her that old Georgie-boy wasn't coming back. The rental agent only had contact details for Herb Vissing, and I'd already closed off that avenue.

"Can you show me your passport, please?" I asked, during what was to be our last sexual encounter (although she couldn't possibly have known that).

"My passport? Why do you ask this, George?"

"Well," I began, shyly. "It's because . . .'

"Yes?"

'Well, I suppose I should be honest and say that I need your passport number to apply for a marriage license in Memphis. You're not an American citizen."

"Memphis?" Her jaw dropped. "We will be married in Memphis? It is incredible, no?" She was laughing now, and then crying the first set of actual tears of joy I think I'd ever seen.

"Yes, Carmen. You see, I had hoped it would be a surprise, but I am confident that the family will allow us to have the wedding reception in Graceland."

"Grace-land," she stuttered. It was as though I'd gotten her a backstage pass to heaven itself. "Oh, George, George, I love you, I love you, I love you." She threw her arms around my neck and kissed me all over my face. Once she'd calmed down, I noted her passport number and her family name (Morel), and tucked the information into my wallet for immediate future reference. I put a call through to Charlie Nagy in the CIA from the phone booth outside the hotel on my way back from the bakery.

"Hey, George, what's new? Need some more autographs tested? Who is it this time, Shirley Temple?"

I laughed. "No, nothing like that, but in fact that information became very useful pretty recently."

"Glad to hear it, George. I'm always happy to do a favor for an old University-of-San-José man."

"So am I, Charlie, and in fact, that's why I'm calling. I'm on vacation in France for a few weeks and I've got a little piece of information which may be of use to you guys."

"Oh yeah? Tell me more, George, I'm interested."

"Well, I don't know if it's anything, but I was in a bar here and I got talking to this couple; and over a few drinks tongues loosened and you know the way people start maybe speaking a little too freely?"

"Yeah? Like how freely, George?"

"Well, that's the thing, Charlie. This girl, all sweet, like cheesecake wouldn't melt in her mouth, she produces her passport to prove who she is, and then she asks me if I would be interested in helping them establish contacts in the States to raise funds for their campaign."

"What campaign, George?" I had Charlie's interest now, alright.

"Something strange, let me think . . . oh yes, I remember. They're called the Liberation Front for an Independent Provence with European Union Funding and Reduced Public Transport Delays."

"Jesus-H, that sounds like heavy shit. Did they mention any other organizations that they have connections with?"

"Hmm, she did mention something about some crew that separates baskets."

"Baskets?"

"Yeah, from Italy or maybe Spain."

"Oh fuck, George. You mean the Basque separatists in Spain?"

"That could be it, Charlie. Any help to you?"

"Oh God, yes, George. The boys upstairs in Counterterrorism are going to be very interested in this. Anything else you can tell me?"

"Well, nothing really, except for her name and passport number, if that's any help?" I could barely stop myself from laughing out loud now. I gave him the details.

"Oh, George, you're absolutely amazing. This is great stuff. You better be careful yourself. I'd advise you to have no further contact with this person or her associates."

"My thoughts exactly, Charlie. Tell me, what will happen to her? I mean she seemed to be planning on visiting the U.S. pretty soon, so, like, can you have her followed or something?"

"Let me put it to you this way, George. If this dame uses that passport, or if that's her real name—and it may well be— then she won't get past Immigration. Even if she does, she'll be picked up by our operatives within twenty-four hours and shipped back to the Independent Railway Republic or wherever, faster than you can say Iraq oil. You know those bastards wouldn't let us use their airspace in . . ."

"Gotta go, Charlie," I cut across him as the beeps began to get louder and faster and my money ran out. It would be the best value for a couple of coins I ever spent. I was pretty sure of that.

Iska phoned on Friday.

"Avignon is great, Dad. We've been all over the place. The food is wonderful and Michel has come down to join us for two days. We found this wonderful church. It's so tiny, and it's right in the middle of a bridge that only goes halfway. Oh, Dad, this has been our best holiday ever. Can we come back?"

"We'll see, honey. We'll see."

"Anyway, we're back to Gigondas tomorrow. Grandma has been a bit quiet, but I think she's enjoying herself, though she seems to be tired all the time. See you tomorrow, Dad."

"See you tomorrow, honey," I said, handing the phone to her mother.

I bet old Muriel was down in the dumps for a bit after our set-to in the front room, but at least the air had been cleared and we both knew where we stood. I was so glad that I hadn't blown the whistle on her with Pearl or the kids. To be honest, I don't think I ever would have. That kind of threat is always much more potent when it's undelivered. Once the cat is out of the bag (or off the farm), the desired effect may not be achieved, or it may be diluted. I was pretty sure I knew Pearl well enough to know that, faced with the information about each of us, she would still have chosen Muriel over me. Maybe Pearl loved me, but she was scared of her mother, and in my experience fear always wins out over love. No, that card was played at just the right time.

I still couldn't believe how lucky I'd been. I knew the old bat would crank up the volume again sometime, and it would be impossible for her to ever completely hold her tongue. But I think I knew that she would never risk my wrath by disclosing my affair with the "pastry puffer." She wouldn't have been able to live with the fallout of Pearl finding out that Louie wasn't her real father. If Pearl ever found out about Carmen I knew that, even if I could prove that Muriel was the Boston Strangler, my marriage would still be over. In any event, Pearl and I were back on track now and in a couple of days we'd be home. Our marriage and my law firm would remain intact, untouched, and ready to roll into the future while G.B.H. reaped the rewards on both fronts.

I worried for a few moments on that Friday night, about Carmen gaining access to my real address in Boston through Michel's contact with Iska. What of it, I thought finally, as I drifted from semi-sleep into half-action as Pearl returned from the bathroom and slipped her nightdress off to reveal the Las Vegas lingerie ensemble. The CIA would clean up the doggie-doo long before it achieved its destination of my doorstep.

Somewhere, early the next day in the midst of a bizarre dream, in which nubile bakers were covering themselves in different flavored cream while the marriage counselor stood outside the window crying, the phone rang. I realized it was a real phone and I woke and picked up the bedside receiver.

"Yes, hello?"

"'Allo? Is this Mr. Henry?"

"Yes, yes. This is George Baxter Henry," I replied, still halfway through licking one of the iced bakers.

"This is the Centre Au Fond du Monde in the Camargue. Your son Beelly came here today."

"Yes? Can I talk to Billy?" I said.

"No," said the voice. "You cannot speak to Beelly. I am sorry, but there's been an accident."

Fenouillet   De La Chine :

false France ; known 1883.

Iskaz . A.

CHAPTER TEN

I drove like a lunatic from Provence to the Camargue but, let me tell you, that's nothing in a country where everyone drives like a lunatic. There are more people killed on the French roads every year than died of TB in France in the whole of the last century. How about that for a statistic? Now, either they knew how to tackle TB ahead of the rest of the world, or they have an outrageous level of road carnage. Each way you slice it, it's pretty impressive. I remember seeing a survey somewhere that said most car accidents happen within six feet of the home, or was it six miles? I have to say that I found that statistic less than impressive. I mean, hey, you spend most of your time at home, so if there's an accident to be had, chances are you'll be around for it and available to take part. Anyway, I drove pretty hard in Olivia's husband's car. As we left Gigondas, I saw Carmen sitting on the steps outside the bakery thumbing through what looked like a bridal magazine. There was absolutely no way I was ever going to buy that house now.

The guy on the phone hadn't said much about the circumstances of the accident, or how Billy was; only that he was now in a hospital in a town called Aigues Mortes. Of course, when he'd told me the name of the place, I'd panicked and thought he was describing Billy's condition. Olivia phoned them back to get the details of where the hospital was, and by eight thirty AM we were on our way. The hospital had given little enough information over the phone, so we were pretty much in the dark.

I was worried as hell. I thought that I would never forgive myself if anything happened to Billy. It would have all been my fault for signing that goddamn consent form and for getting him off the cocaine. It took us just under three hours to get there, and after a couple of wrong turns on roundabouts I found the 'hopital' (as they insist on spelling it). Pearl must have guessed what I was going through and laid no blame on me during the drive down.

"We're looking for our son, Billy," I said to the receptionist.

"Where is he?" She replied with a question.

"How the hell do we know where he is? That's why I'm asking you," I roared. Pearl put a hand on my arm to calm me.

"M'sieu and Madame Henry?" a voice from behind cut across the misunderstanding.

"Yes?" we said, both turning round at the same time. A doctor in a white coat with a stethoscope around his neck beckoned us with his hand like a traffic cop.

"How is he?" I spluttered.

"Is he okay?" Pearl enquired. The guy ignored our questions and simply turned and began to walk purposefully away.

"Please follow me," he said, and so we did.

I gotta tell you that I had skedaddled through every emotion from shit-scared to 'why me?' and back in our drive down from Gigondas. Pearl was worried too, but she remained as calm as hell. Come to think of it, she's never been one to panic. I didn't know if Billy had survived the crash or whether he would be permanently disabled or brain dead, or anything at all. That's parenthood for you—you raise them to fend for themselves, just so that you can continue to worry about them when they become adults. When they're small, you wipe their nose or put a Band-Aid on their knee and watch over them twenty-four seven. Every door-hinge is a potential guillotine. When they're even smaller than that, just babies, you watch over them at night in their cribs and wake them up just to make sure they're only asleep. It's crazy. They grow up, and then it's worse because you don't see them most of the time, but you still worry.

They never worry about you. They just get big enough to know that you still worry about them, and then they use that as leverage for, like, more fucking money or later nights out. Who am I, the goddamn tooth fairy? (Well, I used to be). We followed the doctor until he stopped at the room marked with a sign saying "Morgue," and my heart pressed the button for the basement of my stomach. Pearl took my hand and squeezed it. The doctor buzzed the door, and a nurse peered out of an office window and handed him a chart.

"This way," he said. I closed my eyes and wished I were dead myself. I pushed the door.

"No, no, M'sieu, not that way."

I opened my eyes and saw that he'd begun going up the short flight of stairs to another wing of the hospital altogether. I sighed with relief and felt an irresistible urge to fart, but was afraid under the conditions that I might follow through. So I sucked in my stomach and tried to reverse the traffic. A body in the first bed was covered from head to toe in a plaster cast.

"Hi, Mom, Hi, Dad," Billy called from another bed across the room. His arm was in a sling, and he was sitting up enjoying a pretty healthy looking lunch.

"Oh God, Billy, are you alright?" I said, rushing over to him. "Your mother was worried half to fucking death." Pearl got to him first and kissed him on the cheeks.

"Well, I'd like more orange juice, but apart from that, I'm fine," he said, grinning at me.

Billy let me catch my breath and then, as we sat beside him and ate dry bread and apples, he explained what had happened.

"The adventure place was incredible. I nearly lost my mind during the whole thing."

"You nearly lost your life," I reminded him.

"Steady on, Dad. I'm here, aren't I?"

"Just-a-fucking-'bout," I said. "What the hell went wrong?"

"I got there at lunchtime yesterday. They made me do this medical. They did all kinds of fitness tests, even a brain scan."

"Don't tell me. They scanned but found nothing?"

"Hey, Dad, save it for the Oscars. They had this showroom with every car imaginable and I picked out a brand new Ferrari. Then they brought me to, like, a small cinema and showed me the options."

"The options?"

"Yeah, Dad. There were dozens of wild things to do, but I chose this adventure called Fly Dive."

"I don't want to hear the details," Pearl said, as she stood up. "You're not badly injured, and that's all I need to know. Tell your dad all about it if you want, but I'm going for a walk."

"Fly dive?" I asked, as the door of the hospital ward creaked closed behind my wife.

"Oh, yeah. The kick about Fly Dive is that I got to drive the car at a hundred and seventy miles an hour on a disused stretch of highway about thirty miles long. At the end, the road just stops in midair and I drove the car off it into a lake."

"Into a real lake?" This was incredible.

"Oh no, Dad, not a real lake. An artificial lake, but still with lots of water, just no fish."

"And you drove the car into the lake? Are you fucking crazy? Wouldn't it have been cheaper to buy a sledgehammer and break your arm in the comfort of your own home?"

"Relax, Dad, it's all covered. The lake is only a couple of yards deep and they've got frogmen standing by to rescue you once you hit the water."

"Why don't they just get you to stop the car before the road ends? That way you wouldn't run the risk of drowning."

"You don't get it, do you, Dad?"

"Get what? What's to get? You're almost killed driving a fast car into a fucking pond; that's not so hard to understand." I was furious now, as well as relieved.

"Cool it, Dad, it's okay. These guys are professionals; they hauled me out of there in less than two minutes. I was just a little bit wet that's all. I had nearly a whole minute to spare before the car exploded."

"Exploded? Is that how you broke your arm? Some of the debris?"

"Oh this?" he said, wagging his sling. "Nah, I fell, climbing up the steps to the office to pay my bill after the rescue."

"You paid for this? Are you crazy? How much?"

"Fifteen, Dad."

"Fifteen hundred bucks?" I couldn't believe it.

"No, Dad, fifteen thousand." He grinned.

"Are you out of your fucking mind, Billy? Are you sure you're not mistaken?"

"'We all got to cut loose sometime and make our own mistakes,' remember that, Dad?"

"Who said that?"

"You did."

"When?"

"That day we made the deal."

I'd remembered the phrase immediately he'd said it, but had hoped he'd forgotten where he'd heard it.

"I never said that, Billy," I said, but as I did, I knew that both of us knew I was lying. I took a couple of deep breaths and looked at my son and laid some truth on him. "You scared the fuck out of me and your mom, Billy. I thought you were dead or paralyzed or something. This guy phoned in the middle of the night and—"

"I'm not dead, Dad," he said with a smirk.

"I can fucking well see that," I said. "That's why I'm so mad at you."

"Because I'm not dead?"

"Yes. No. I mean, yes, I'm mad but not because—damn it, Billy, don't ever scare me like this again. I let you out of my sight for an instant and this happens. Jesus, you could have been killed. Do these guys have permits to do this—training, licenses?"

"Absolutely, Dad. It's very, very safe. The statistics show that you're safer here than you'd probably be in your own home."

"Bullshit, Billy."

"No, Dad, really. You know what the chances are that something awful would happen, like say, being punched in the face and knocked off a roof into a swimming pool when you're out of your head on drugs?"

"Okay, okay," I said. "I get the picture. Let's phone Iska and tell her you're okay. We left a note for her in the house for when she gets back from Avignon."

"I already did that, Dad, first thing this morning. I called their hotel in Avignon and talked to her and Grandma."

"So when we were driving down here, worried sick about whether you'd even survived, everyone else knew you were okay, is that what you're telling me?"

"Uh huh."

"For God sakes, Billy, what's wrong with you? You live two different lives at the same time. In one life, your poor fucking father—namely mutt-face, yours truly—and your long-suffering mother are driving, probably even faster than you did yesterday, thinking you might be dead; and meanwhile, the rest of the family is packing to go home knowing you're safe and sound. Is that right?"

"That's right, Dad. But it's not deliberate. I couldn't reach you while you were driving."

"And that makes it okay?"

"That makes it human, Dad. These things happen. It's not like I knowingly fed you and Mom different information so that you wouldn't know what was happening, while I kept Iska and Grandma in the loop."

"Billy, if you knowingly did that, I'd rip your head off. Would you even understand why?"

"Sure, Dad. I mean, that would be like having an affair behind someone's back and pretending all the time that you loved them. Right, Dad?"

"Exactly, Billy . . ." My voice slowed to silence. Who did I think I was, moralizing to my son in a hospital in France? I might as well just qualify as a surgeon and take the 'Hypocrisy Oath.' Billy looked at me and smiled.

"I gotta get to the airport, Dad. The awards ceremony is in less than twelve hours."

Pearl arrived with two big bunches of grapes, and Billy and I devoured every last one. One of the nurses had a pretty decent pair of peaches herself.

Billy made his flight with very little time to spare, and Pearl and I checked in for two nights at the Hotel Grand Aston in the centre of Nice. Iska and Muriel met us at the airport on Sunday. Olivia's husband had driven them and all of our luggage in a rental car, and then picked up his own from me at the car park outside the departures lounge. I expected Iska to be heartbroken about having to leave her first real boyfriend behind.

"Hey, no way, Dad. It's cool. Michel is coming over to Boston for Christmas to stay with us. It was Grandma's idea."

Over the previous forty-eight hours, I'd had a bit of time to do some thinking. I gotta say that I'm not much usually for thinking, but in a way, that period of time, between waving Billy goodbye and meeting Iska and the others before our own flight, was no bad thing. I had felt really close to Pearl on the trip down in the car. I mean we were right beside each other in the fucking car, but you know what I mean. On our last night in France, eating out at a restaurant where they served steak and French fries, some piece of the jigsaw had slotted into place as I watched Pearl return from the restroom and approach our table. I realized in that instant, as she sidestepped a waiter carrying a tray of wine glasses over his head, that this was my wife, this was my life, and I was better off than millions of other guys all over the world who still had their heads halfway up their asses.

"You look very pleased with yourself, George," Pearl said, as she sat down opposite me.

"I *am* pleased," I said. "I'm pleased to be able to say that, even after all these years, you're still the best thing that's ever happened to me." Pearl smiled, and in that smile I saw the girl who had captured my heart in the days before the oil crisis threw everything upside-down. It was great to be alive.

I suppose that, really, it was the drive down to the hospital, when we didn't know how Billy was, that had started the grey cells cavorting with each other. In that frame of existence, trapped in someone else's car in another country in the stifling heat, I had thought about death for the first time. Now, don't get me wrong, I've seen death before. I mean, as a lawyer you get to go to lots of funerals. But thinking about the end of the life of a child you've raised. Well, that's different.

With Iska's twin, there had been absolutely nothing we could have done to prevent her death; but I'd gotten Billy from kindergarten to *Playboy* without ever dreaming for a second that he wouldn't outlast me. Even when Billy was in the Olympic Snorting Team, I never thought he'd die. I figured the worst that would happen would be that maybe he'd never hold down a job, or he'd vote Democrat, or go fucking sterile or something. And then, before I knew he was okay, I imagined all kinds of horrible things that I'd never had to face before. It made me stop and think of my own life and of how I was spending it.

"Are you okay, George?" Pearl placed a hand on my arm as some twit in a uniform weighed the bags at the check-in desk the following day.

"Of course, I'm okay, Pearl. I'm on my way home from my vacation to six weeks worth of paperwork. Why shouldn't I be okay?"

"Oh, nothing," she replied. "You just seem, well, I don't know. A bit subdued or something. Are you sure you're alright?" She kissed me on the cheek with the tenderness of a lover, which was a sensation I'd almost forgotten.

"Pearl, I'm gonna sit with my granddaughter on this flight," Muriel said. "She's going to let me read her manuscript about apples." Muriel edged ahead of me in the line. She handed in her ticket and passport with one hand and held Iska's arm with the other.

I watched these three generations of women and, for the first time ever, saw a clear resemblance in the jawlines and in the eyes. I thought about Carmen and her bridal magazine, thumbing her way into the future in a rush of choices between off-white and light blue. What the fuck was I doing with my life? How many lives was I trying to live? I wondered if the CIA was already circulating her passport number to all ports and airports. You know, I began to feel guilty about Carmen. I mean, she hadn't done anything wrong; I was the one who was cheating on someone as we humped our way through her record collection. I suddenly thought, for no apparent reason, about my honeymoon with Pearl in 1976 and the Elvis concert we'd attended in Indianapolis the following year. I remembered Pearl screaming when he'd arrived onstage, to the "Also Sprach Zarathustra" riffs. Somewhere back there, twenty-odd years ago, we'd had some great times and had each rebounded sufficiently strongly to form one fucking bouncy marriage together. I wondered what life would be like without her, but I didn't really want to think about that much, so I didn't.

"Hey, George, we'll miss the plane if you don't hurry," Pearl shouted to me from one of the duty-free cashier desks, as she bought perfume while I idled in the whiskey section and chose nothing.

"I wonder how Billy got on at the awards ceremony," Iska said, as I was caught in a traffic jam in the aisle of the plane behind some guy with an ass the size of New Jersey.

"I don't know how he expected to play the drums with his arm in a sling," I muttered.

"He told me they were gonna set it up so he only had one drum and they'd make a big deal out of his accident," she said back.

I imagined old Goose Silverspoon and the boys in the publicity department lapping that up.

"What song were they performing?" Pearl asked from behind me.

"Something about cats," I said, turning slightly, to look at her over my shoulder.

"Oh," she said, and blushed. Only the previous day, while we were sightseeing in Nice, we'd discussed the gestures she'd made to me when I'd been up on the roof trying to stop Billy from committing suicide.

"I was trying to signal to you about that song they have called 'Sheriff and the Posse,'" she said. She'd been highly embarrassed when I'd explained.

The in-flight entertainment consisted of the usual fucking assortment of films, which I had either seen hundreds of times before or had deliberately avoided.

"It's always the same," I complained, as Pearl settled down to listen to some classical music on the radio headset.

"What? Did you say something, George?" She lifted the earpiece closest to me for a second.

"I said, it's always the same."

"What's always the same, George?"

"The goddamn movies they show on these goddamn flights. It's always some stupid cop story with clever dogs and a police chief who stands in his office with his sleeves rolled up shouting at the main character, 'You better not screw up on this or you're finished,' or, 'You're off the case, just let the guys at Homicide do their job.'"

A lady passing by to go to the can stopped and stared at us as I spoke the lines. She looked horrified.

"Oh, George. Why don't you just put the eye mask on and go to sleep." Pearl resumed her enjoyment of Ludwig Van Mozart, or whoever.

I must have drifted off to sleep pretty shortly after that because I don't even remember tuning out from the movie. In my exhausted fucking trancelike rest, I had the strangest dream. In it, I flew over Graceland, wearing nothing but the eagle cape. Down below me, I could see someone driving a car toward the swimming pool. As I got closer, there was a crowd of people all wearing baker's hats and applauding as the car crept closer to the pool. I strained to see the driver and I think I expected it to be Billy. Only it wasn't—it was Pearl. I tried to call out to her as a group of frogmen filed out of the pool house one after another, thumbing through bridal magazines as they walked. Somewhere behind me, a voice was calling. At first it sounded like Gloria. She was hysterical.

'George, George. The plumber still hasn't come back to fix my boiler.' Her voice morphed into the muffled laugh of the cops in the station. 'Hey, Barney, it's Gloria Dinerclub's sugar daddy.' I was right over the pool now, and as I hovered about three or four feet from the water, it turned to glass; and then the glass slid back to reveal Billy in a nurse's uniform handing me a clipboard. 'This way, M'sieu and Madame Henry,' he said. 'The doctor is waiting, the doctor is waiting, the doctor . . .'

"Is there a doctor on board?" The announcement woke me, and I blinked as I lifted the eye mask and saw that most people around me were awake and eating some plastic food. "Please make yourself known to one of the cabin crew."

"Mrs. Henry?" A stewardess blocked the aisle and spoke to Pearl.

"Yes?" Pearl looked up from the in-flight magazine and an article about mineral water from the Rockies.

"Could you please come up to row seventeen—your mother has asked for you. Please hurry."

Pearl immediately understood the urgency of the situation and sprung into action. As I let her out, I thought to myself, oh fuck, the old bat is about to kick the bucket and wants to make sure it's full of shit to pour over yours truly after she's gone.

We were half an hour from New York and no emergency landing was possible. I watched helplessly as a makeshift curtain was put up around my mother-in-law at forty thousand feet. Some off-duty doctor tried to haul her back from eternity with mouth-to-mouth. Iska came down the aisle to sit with me.

"Is she going to be alright, Dad? She just suddenly went all funny and grabbed at her throat."

"She just skipped the line" is what I wanted to say but didn't. The paramedics were on the plane like lightning when we touched down. A couple of shakes of the head, like in the movies, and my wife was an orphan. As we left the plane, Pearl was distraught. I hugged her as tightly as I could.

"She's gone, George. She's gone," she sobbed.

"I know, I know."

Iska came to join us, and she and Pearl held hands leaving the plane. This was a poignant symmetry to her actions six hours earlier when she'd linked arms with her grandmother at the check-in desk in Nice. As we walked down the short corridor to the electric walkway, I looked at Pearl to see if I could get an inkling of what had passed between her mother and herself before death had gate-crashed their conversation. I could learn nothing. As we entered the baggage claim area, a guy wheeling a trolley past us unfolded the *New York Times* and took out the sports section—abandoning the rest on a counter where some lazy airline lady was biting her nails. My son, Billy, looked up at me from the front page in a photo, where he played a single drum with one hand and proudly displayed his other arm in a sling.

ARM IN A SLING, HEAD IN THE CLOUDS, NUMBER ONE IN THE CHARTS, the headline read.

I was surrounded by my family in the fucking baggage claim area in JFK, with Iska and Pearl looking for our luggage somewhere behind me, and Billy on the front page in my hands. Sometime—in between Billy's head being in the toilet over the Azores and this discarded newspaper—in six weeks I'd found out something about myself. Nothing fancy or philosophical, or religious or profound. But something so glaringly fucking simple that the only amazing thing about it was that it had taken fifty-one years for me to realize it. We're all gonna die someday, and in between being born and then, you only have one fucking life. If you spend more time being happy with what you've got than you do being unhappy about things you don't have, then you've cracked the secret.

·············⟨⟨⟨⟨⟩⟩⟩⟩·············

Billy's gonna be twenty next week. East Pole are in the middle of recording the difficult third album, and Billy's dating some broad who's just made a movie and is tipped for an Oscar next year. What is it about this family and Best Supporting actresses? Iska's still at school, but her book has been published and sold a couple of thousand copies. Now she's working on one about different varieties of beetroot. God only knows what she'll do when she gets to Q.

I heard from Charlie Nagy at a class reunion last November. Carmen tried to brazen her way into the country some time back. Some people never give up. She was turned back at JFK with the sad news from a field operative that her intended had been tragically killed in a freak shaving accident just days after I'd returned from France. I got one of the junior partners in a law firm in Memphis to forward $20,000 and a hamburger cookbook as her share of my estate. I guess she has a heart of gold and I just broke it. I sure hope it mends.

The translation service upstairs from Schwartz, McNaghten, Stamp and Henry have moved, and a male impotency clinic has taken their place. Their slogan is, 'If you can rise up to the ninth floor, anything is possible.'

And me? Am I happy? Who's ever fucking happy? I'm a bit older and maybe not much wiser, but I'll tell you one thing, I'm probably less of a malcontent than I was, and that's something. The woman who had my children, and who's put up with me for over a quarter of a century, is the only woman for me and I think I've finally realized that. I've gone almost three years now without even thinking about being unfaithful (unless you count the internet chat room thing with Angeline from Dallas who turned out to be a guy when I phoned her; in which case it's only two years, nine months). Business is booming and

I'm healthy except for hemorrhoids, peeing more often than I want to, and finding it a bit hard to hear TV sometimes. We took that trip of a lifetime Billy had paid for with his advance, and there's a photograph on my bedside table of the four of us outside Graceland. We've got tickets to see the Korgis' second 'final reunion concert' on New Year's Eve next at the Boston Coliseum. I hope to stay around long enough to see their next 'final reunion concert,' whenever that is.

I never did find out whether Muriel got to tell Pearl about my dough rising with the bakery lady, but in a way it just doesn't matter anymore. What has happened has happened and you can't change it, but you can change the future and that's what I'm trying to do. I'm crankier now than Henry Fonda was in the film *On Golden Lake*, but at least it's contented cranky instead of demented cranky. Nobody really makes you do anything, it's all inside your own fucking head, the choices, the answers, hey, even the questions.

I think about Muriel every once in a while whenever I hear Elvis on the radio, and I imagine the two of them somewhere arguing the toss about the best version of "Suspicious Minds." I guess I even miss her a little now she's gone, but, let me tell you, she was impossible to miss when she was here.

I don't think I'll ever go back to France, but who cares about that? Not me. We had a good time there and maybe that place can even take a little of the credit for straightening out old GBH and family. Yeah, I guess it can. But you gotta draw the line somewhere. As old Dubya Bush says, "Those guys in France don't even have a word in their language for entrepreneur."

How could you trust a fucking country like that?

<u>Unless</u> the tree is exeptionly damaged
and <u>very</u> <u>old</u>, it is rarely so
depilitated that it cannot be
Saved !!!!

Lots of Love
Iska Henry.